JOE RUCKER

AN UNADJUSTEDS STORY

MARISA NOELLE

CONTENT WARNINGS

This book contains themes and references that some readers may find distressing, including, but not limited to:

Violence – Physical fights and injuries.

Death – Characters dying, sometimes in graphic or emotionally intense ways.

Torture/Abuse – Physical or psychological torture or abusive power dynamics.

Oppression – Totalitarian regimes, discrimination, or forced conformity.

Rebellion/Anarchy – Destructive acts, rebellion against authority, or revolution.

Imprisonment/Enslavement – Characters held against their will, enslaved, or confined.

Manipulation/Brainwashing – Mind control or forced ideological conformity.

Mental Health Issues – Depression, PTSD, anxiety.

Body Horror/Mutations – Genetic modifications, experiments, or body mutilations.

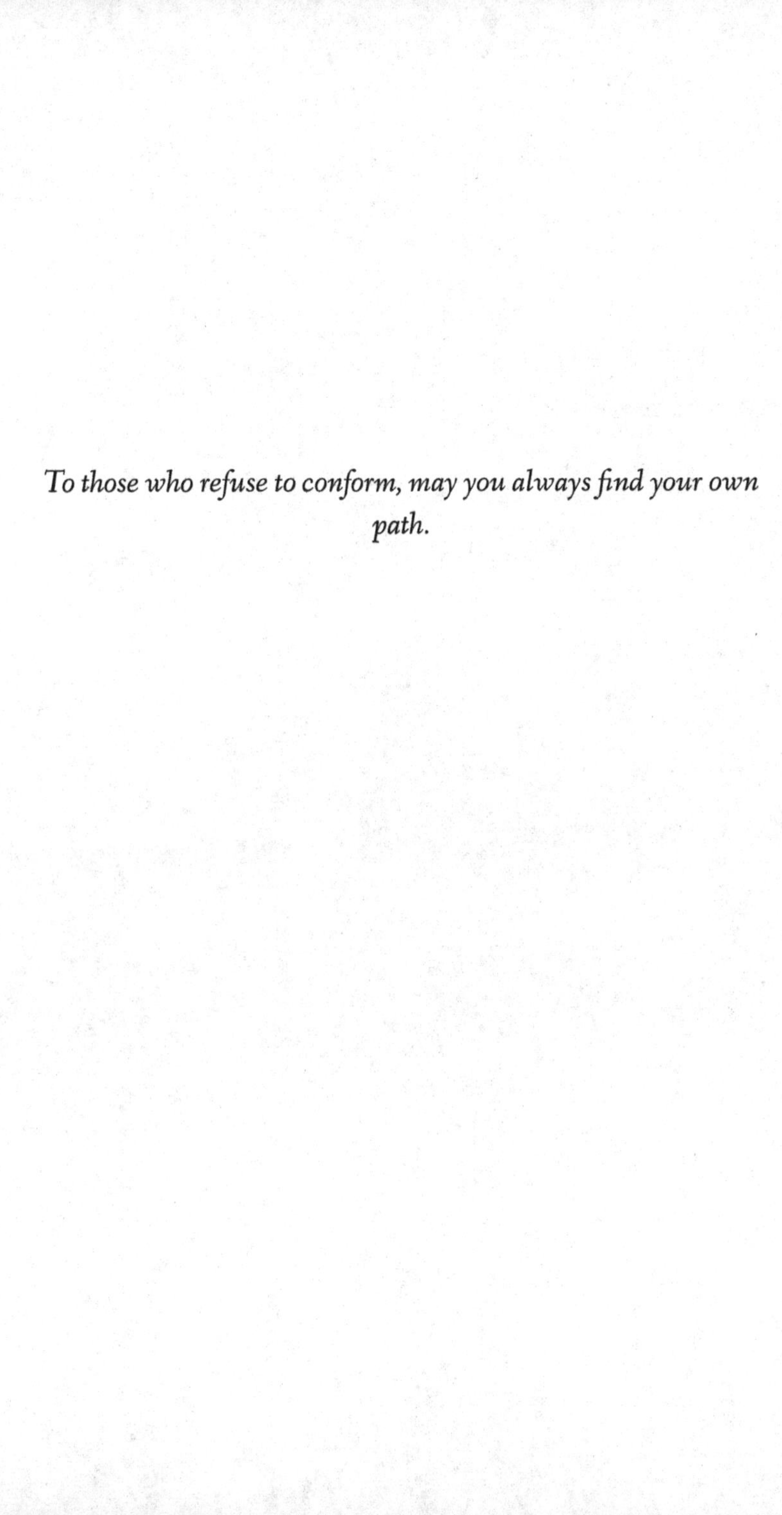

To those who refuse to conform, may you always find your own path.

CHAPTER 1

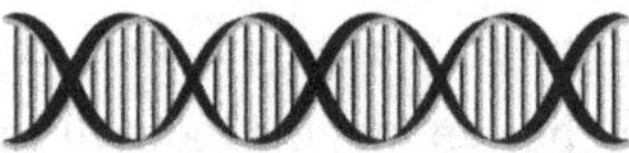

Joe works out the kinks in his muscles from the battering he took yesterday. Half his team are bulks, and he ended up underneath a pile of them. If he doesn't start playing more defensively, he might not see the end of the season.

"It's time!" His mom calls him through to the kitchen.

He limps through the doorway, glad of a couple days off from training to recover. He'll have to scrounge more tape from the medical office, not that tape will be much defense against a bulk with armored skin and increased strength.

Joe settles himself at the kitchen table, a lopsided cake with a few flickering candles before him. His mom and dad hover nearby, their eyes shining with anticipation.

"Make a wish, son," his dad says, his voice gruff.

Joe closes his eyes, takes a deep breath, and allows all his dreams to float through his mind. He skims through the ones that aren't possible. The big things. The ones he has no control over and concentrates on something a little smaller.

He blows the candle out. Smoke curls toward the stained ceiling as his parents clap and cheer.

"Sixteen already," Joe's mom says. She pulls him into a tight hug, her flowery perfume enveloping him.

The comment sends a pang of anxiety to flutter in his chest. *Sixteen.* He's one of only three players on the varsity football team who haven't taken a nanite. If he doesn't get his hands on one soon, he can kiss his football career goodbye.

"I'll be gray before you know it." He covers his anxiety with a joke as he rakes a hand through his lengthening blond hair.

His parents laugh, but it doesn't ring true. Joe gives them a once over, notes how they're both perched on the edge of their seats as if they might suddenly be ejected by hidden springs.

"What is it?" he asks.

They share a look. A look that brings genuine smiles to both their faces. Joe tries to relax, but he's so used to being tense all the time, waiting for a blow to land on him, that he struggles to let go.

"Mom? Dad?"

His dad clears his throat. "Son, we know how much football means to you. How you dream of making it to the NFL."

Joe nods, his heart swelling. All he's ever wanted is to play pro ball...to hear the roar of the crowd as he sprints for the end zone.

"Well, we wanted to give you something special for your birthday," his mom says. "Something to help make that dream a reality."

Joe's thoughts spiral. There's only one thing he's ever wished for. The exact same wish for every birthday for as long as he can remember. Dammit. He was supposed to concentrate on the small things. The things that might just be possible. But the thing he really wants always pops into his head as he blows the candles out. Every year. But there is no way in hell is parents can afford it.

His dad hands him a small box wrapped in paper that's seen better days. "We know you'll make it, champ," he says, his tone lighter than it's been in years.

Joe stares at the small box, his palms slickening and his mouth drying out. He wasn't expecting a present. They agreed a long time ago that a cake was enough. Being together. Maybe taking in a movie.

"What is it?" he asks, glancing at his parents.

"Open it," his mom says.

Tentatively, Joe reaches for the small box and unwraps the gift to reveal a single pill, no larger than a bean, but it's what it represents that makes his heart thunder in his chest.

"Is this what I think it is?" Joe asks, his gaze darting between his parents.

They both smile and nod.

"We can't afford this," Joe says, not daring to touch the pill, not daring to see if it's actually real.

His mom's eyes glisten. "We've been saving for months to get this for you. Because we believe in you, Joe. We know you have what it takes to go all the way."

Joe swallows hard, overwhelmed by emotion. They've already sacrificed so much for him—worked extra shifts, helped him with his homework when the numbers in his math paper kept spinning in circles, attended every one of his football games. And now this.

He picks up the bulk nanite pill, rolling it between his fingers. Such a tiny thing, yet it holds the key to his future. To making all their dreams come true.

"Guys, this must've cost—" Joe starts, but his mom cuts him off with a wave of her hand.

"Your career is worth every penny," she says, her smile bright, but Joe is aware of the expense, of how little they have in their savings account. He casts a look around the apartment. It's clean and tidy, most of the furniture second hand. Nothing matches. Hand-me-downs and chipped china. The coffee table now more nicks than wood. Gouges in the architraves from throwing a ball around when he was a kid. But it is home.

A cold sweat erupts over his skin as the pill settles in his palm. It's everything he ever wanted.

"I don't know what to say," he murmurs.

"You don't have to say anything. We're giving you this because we're proud of you." His dad claps him on the back. "You focus on football and leave the rest to us."

Joe nods, renewed determination surging through him. With his parents' love and this nanite enhancing his natural abilities, nothing can stop him now. He'll make it to the NFL, no matter what it takes. For them.

"Imagine the headlines," his dad says, excitement warming his tone. "'Joe Rucker, youngest player to be drafted into the NFL.'"

For a moment, a flicker of uncertainty crosses his mind. Is this really the right path? But he quickly pushes the thought away. Of course it is. There is no other way. He'll be crushed and killed on the field if he doesn't take it.

"Aren't you going to take it?" his mom asks.

Joe cradles the nanite in his palm, feeling the weight of his future balanced on the edge of this tiny technological marvel. He knows this is more than just a birthday present; it's his family's legacy. And with it, he's determined to give them the world, or at least a decent-sized chunk of Kansas, maybe starting with a car that works and an apartment where they don't hear the report of gunfire in the middle of the night. Once he gets drafted, that is.

Joe slips the pill into his mouth and swallows it with a swig of water. The die is cast. His future awaits. A hot flush skates over his skin.

A hush of silence follows as his parents stare at him.

Then it begins.

A tingling sensation races through Joe's veins, like he's connected to the smallest of electrical currents. His muscles spasm and convulse as the nanites go to work, rewriting his DNA, restructuring him from the inside out. He doubles over, gasping, as pain lances through his core.

"Joe!" His mom reaches for him, alarmed, but he waves her off.

"I'm okay," he grits out between clenched teeth. "I think...it's working."

Even as he speaks, he can feel the changes taking hold. His limbs elongate, bones thickening and strengthening. Muscles bulge and ripple beneath his skin, swelling with newfound power. The fibers of his shirt strain against his expanding frame, then tear with a loud rip. He stands, and as he does, the room seems to shrink around him.

Joe staggers to his feet, marveling at the sheer size of his hands, the dense bulk of his arms and chest. He's always been tall for his age, but now he towers over his parents, easily eight feet of pure, sculpted muscle.

"Whoa," he breathes, flexing experimentally. The casual motion nearly puts his fist through the wall. "This is unreal." His voice booms with a deep resonance that vibrates against the thin apartment walls.

His skin hardens, becoming a living armor that no bullet can penetrate. The sensation is bizarre; like wearing a suit tailored not from fabric, but from resilience itself. He is now fire-retardant too, but the idea of testing that sends a flare of alarm flickering down his spine.

"Fire resistant and bulletproof," his dad murmurs in awe. "Just like they promised."

Joe barely hears him, too caught up in the sheer rush of power thrumming through his transformed body. He feels invincible, unstoppable. Like he could take on the entire world and win.

Grinning, he grabs his football and spins it on one finger, relishing the perfect balance and control. His mind races ahead, envisioning the speed and agility waiting to be unleashed on the field.

No one will be able to touch him. He'll shatter every record, lead his team to championship after championship. And with the signing bonuses and endorsement deals sure to follow, he'll finally be able to give his parents the life they deserve. No more pinching pennies and clipping coupons. Only the best, from here on out.

"I'm going to do it," he declares, clutching the ball tight. Determination blazes through him, bright and unwavering. "I'm going to make it to the NFL. I'm going to be the best damn player they've ever seen."

He meets his parents' eyes, sees his own fierce joy and anticipation mirrored there. "And we'll never have to worry about anything, ever again. I promise."

Best birthday present ever.

In the mirror, golden eyes gaze back at him, set in a face that's still his, yet somehow more.

"Like looking at a superhero," his mom whispers.

"Or the next NFL legend," his dad adds.

The dream unfurls in Joe's mind, vibrant and intoxicating. Stadiums roaring with cheers, the thrill of the game under blinding lights, and the weight of a football secure in his hands.

"I think it's time to cut the cake," his mom says, knife in hand. They gather around the stained coffee table, mismatched forks in hand, ready to dive into the mess his mom baked. She's never professed to excel at baking, or cooking. His dad usually makes most of their meals. But he can't fault her effort.

As his parents cut generous helpings of cake, Joe picks at his own slice, his stomach still roiling from the rapid changes in his body.

His dad digs into his slice. "Just promise you won't forget about us little people when you're rich and famous, yeah?"

"Never," Joe vows, raising his fork in a mock toast. "You'll be right there with me, every step of the way. Front row seats to every game."

In his heart, amidst the armored skin and altered strength, the most human part of Joe swells with purpose. The dreams of his parents, the sacrifices they've made—they're etched into his DNA now, driving him forward. With each beat of his enhanced heart, his confidence grows as he finally believes he can be the one to change their stars.

Joe settles back in the chair, almost snapping a leg, and pours soda for them all. He's careful to hold the glasses gently so as not to shatter them with his newfound strength.

"Sixteen looks good on you, son," his mom says, her smile tender.

"Here's to your future," his dad raises his glass of soda, the fizzing pop of carbonation sounding like miniature fireworks. "To touchdowns and triumphs."

"To making every play count," Joe adds, lifting his own glass. His voice is steady, but inside, there's an echo of uncertainty. What if the dream is too big? What if—

No. He shakes off the doubts, the towering shadow of 'what ifs'. This is his moment, their moment, and nothing—not fear, not the oppressive confines of their apartment, not even the unknown—will taint it.

They clink glasses. For now, the warmth of family and the simple joy of a shared birthday cake are enough. They laugh, they eat, and they pretend, at least for tonight, that the world hasn't shifted beneath their feet.

CHAPTER 2

Three Years Later

JOE STANDS at the edge of the windswept Kansas wheat field, his eight-foot frame casting a long shadow that mingles with the fading sun. It's been three years since the nanites rewrote his DNA, three years since he transformed from an average guy into a hulking mass of muscle and power.

He chuckles to himself, watching his breath form clouds in the crisp air, the irony not lost on him. Once just a guy with golden eyes and corn-colored hair trying to make his mark, now he's a spectacle wherever he goes...thanks to a pill.

Joe's phone buzzes. He glances at the screen—a text from his mom.

We are so proud of you! Can't wait to see your new place. Love you!

A smile spreads across his face. After all their sacrifices, scrimping and saving to buy him that fateful nanite pill, he can finally give back to them. A car that functions and a house of their own, just down the street. It's the least he can do. It may have taken him three years, but he's done it.

He flexes his arm, watching the enhanced muscles ripple under his armored skin. The old Joe is gone, transformed on a molecular level into this hulking "bulk". Inside, he's still the same guy, but with a hell of a lot more power humming through his veins.

The world has changed too, in three short years. Genetic enhancements, once a miracle for the wounded and ill, are now *the* must-have accessory for the elite. As well as the not-so-elite. And those who scramble to find something cheap and uncut on the black market. Sometimes Joe wonders if he's done the right thing. But if he hadn't taken that pill, he and his parents would still be counting coins by a candle in a one-bedroom apartment.

He shakes off the sudden wave of emotion as he turns away from the endless waves of wheat. Joe jumps into the truck he parked on the side of the road and heads back to the stadium. It's not a long drive, but as he cruises along the familiar streets, he allows the sights and smells of his home state to center him. All the things he loves.

Joe arrives at the playing field, flashes his I.D., and saunters into the changing room to greet his teammates. After a few minutes of exchanging testosterone-fueled greetings and pumped-up well-wishes, Joe changes into his kit and begins his pre-game good luck routine. It doesn't take long. Mostly, it's a prayer of thanks. Well, not a prayer, a thought. He thanks his parents for everything they provided him with, and even the things they couldn't. Without their guidance and humility, he wouldn't be the person he is now.

So he mutters his thanks, hoping somehow they know how grateful he is. And if they don't know already, they soon will.

He grins to himself as he charges onto the field. The roar of the crowd echoes in Joe's ears, drowning out any other noise. Adrenaline spikes, bringing a rush of energy. The announcer's voice echoes from the speakers, along with blaring music, which incites the crowd into a roaring frenzy.

As he emerges from the dark tunnel, the scent of freshly cut grass and sweat lingers in the air as he steps onto the turf. He takes a deep breath, the adrenaline pumping through him heightening his senses. He catches a whiff of concession foods being sold in the stands, but his focus is on the game ahead.

There is a metallic taste lingering in Joe's mouth, a mix of nerves and anticipation. He licks his lips. Excitement courses through his veins, causing his heart to pound like a steady battle drum in his chest. A grin spreads across his face as he rolls his shoulders, savoring the sensation of his powerful muscles shifting and flexing beneath his skin.

The first time he had stepped onto the field after the transformation, it had felt foreign and clumsy. Like inhabiting a body that didn't belong to him. But now, after countless hours of training and honing his abilities, he moves with fluid precision. His powerful frame responds effortlessly to his every command, like a well-oiled machine.

The stadium lights are like a thousand fireflies, their luminous dance punctuated by the sharp white lines of the field. Joe's enhanced eyes soak in the vivid details, every blade of grass and bead of sweat on his opponents' faces visible. He pushes himself into a run, the turf beneath him springing back like a trampoline, propelling him forward.

As he jogs toward the huddled mass of his teammates, a familiar lightness bubbles up. The simple joy of the game. The camaraderie of striving together for a shared goal. For a few precious hours, the complications fall away—the stares and whispers that follow him off the field, the knowledge that he'll never be "normal" again. Whatever that word means now. Bulk *is* normal in the football world. He can count the number of unadjusted pro players on one hand.

The team breaks apart and he trots to his position, scanning the defense. His enhanced mental processing allows him to track every opposing player at once, anticipating their movements. As the ball snaps, the world slows. He weaves through grasping hands with preternatural agility, legs pumping like pistons. The wind whips past his face.

The field is a blur of green and white as Joe dashes toward the end zone, his teammates cheering and pumping their fists in the air. After sprinting ninety yards, he finally reaches the end zone and slams the ball into the ground with a triumphant roar. The crowd's cheers ricochet through the stadium, drowning out the sound of his heartbeat. His teammates swarm him, pounding on his back in celebration. A wide grin spreads across his face, almost painful in its intensity. This. This is what he is made for. The taste of victory is sweet on Joe's tongue, and his grin stretches from ear to ear.

The rest of the game passes by in a blur of movement and power, the team functioning as a single, conscious mind. Joe's body moves on instinct, every muscle working in perfect harmony. And when the final whistle blows, the scoreboard tells the story: a resounding victory, with Joe's stats jumping off the page in bold letters. The stadium erupts into a frenzy of cheering and applause, the air electric with excitement and pride. And he isn't even out of breath.

Reporters clamor for interviews as the crowd closes around Joe. His coach pushes through the scrum with a wide grin on his face.

"MVP!" he shouts, raising Joe's hand high. The pride and excitement radiating from him is palpable. "Helluva game, son. Helluva game."

The cheers and applause of the onlookers only add to the moment, making it feel like an electric charge in the air. Joe can't help but smile, knowing this is only the beginning of his journey.

His first professional football game. This is a high like no other. And damn, he needs to celebrate.

Joe strides through the tunnel toward the changing rooms, his helmet tucked under his arm. He feels wired in a way he doesn't think he'll ever come down from.

Coach slaps an arm over his shoulder, his face split in a huge grin. "Joe! Fantastic game out there, my boy. Those touchdown runs were a thing of beauty."

Joe ducks his head, a modest smile playing on his lips. "Thanks, Coach. Just trying to do my part for the team."

"Keep playing like that and we'll be unstoppable this season. But I'll have to keep an eye on you—wouldn't want any other teams trying to poach my star player!"

Joe laughs, shaking his head. "No worries there, Coach. I'm loyal to the bone."

As he makes his way to his locker, Joe can't help but

notice the gaggle of cheerleaders hovering outside the doors to the changing room. They giggle and whisper, their eyes fixed on him with undisguised admiration.

One of them, a stunning blonde with jet-black wings, saunters over to him. "Hey, Joe," she purrs, trailing a perfectly manicured finger along his arm. "Great game today. You were amazing out there."

Joe flashes her a friendly smile, but keeps his tone polite. "Thanks, uh…"

"Tiffany," she supplies, batting her lashes. "I was thinking, maybe we could grab a drink sometime? Celebrate your big win?"

Joe hesitates, his gaze flicking to his teammates. He knows the kind of attention that comes with being a star player, and discomfort wriggles over him tighter than his armored skin.

"I appreciate the offer, Tiffany," he says gently, "but I've got plans with my folks tonight. Rain check?"

Tiffany pouts prettily, but nods. "Sure thing, Joe. You know where to find me." She sashays away, hips swaying.

Joe sighs, running a hand through his sweat-dampened hair. He knows he'll have to get used to this kind of attention, but right now, all he wants is a hot shower and a quiet dinner with his parents.

He thinks about the surprise he's prepared for them. With a small smile, Joe grabs his towel and heads for the showers, ready to wash away the grime of the game and bask in the warm glow of victory and family.

After a quick celebratory drink with his team, Joe meets his parents at their favorite local diner. The worn vinyl booths and familiar scent of greasy fries envelop him like a comforting hug as he slides in across from his mom and dad.

"There's our star player!" His dad beams, his weathered face crinkling with pride. "Thank you for getting us the tickets."

"Of course." Joe ducks his head, a slight flush creeping up his neck. "I've set aside tickets for every game."

His mom reaches across the table to squeeze his hand, her eyes misty. "We're so proud of you, Joe. To see you out there..." She shakes her head as she presses a fingertip to the corner of her eye.

Joe swallows past the sudden lump in his throat. "Couldn't have done it without you two," he says gruffly.

They order their usual—burgers and shakes—and fall into easy conversation, trading stories and laughter like they always have. For a moment, it's like nothing has changed, like Joe is still that scrawny kid from Kansas with big dreams and a bigger heart.

When the moment is right, Joe removes the cluster of keys from his pocket and lays them on the table.

"What's that?" his mom asks.

"Bought yourself a sports car?" His dad's eyes brim.

Joe snorts. "No way. These are for you."

His mom frowns, scans the street. "What am I supposed to do with these?"

Joe tilts his head, suppresses a smile. "Drive your new car." He points out the window at the compact Volvo. It's secondhand, but nearly new, and purrs like a kitten on cat nip.

Her mouth gapes open. His dad sheds a tear.

They venture outside to inspect the car.

"You didn't need to buy us a car," his dad says, running a finger over the paintwork.

Joe knows what he's really thinking. That a new car won't pay the bills stacked on their worn kitchen table. But what they don't know is that this morning, Joe spent a couple of hours at the bank and paid off all their loans and bills.

"Get in," Joe says. "We've got places to be."

His parents exchange a look, but climb into the car. Joe squeezes his bulk into the back seat. He gives them directions and they cruise through the city streets until half an hour later, they arrive in a quieter neighborhood. White picket fences. Tire swings in the front yards. Flower boxes and potted plants lining windows and standing sentry at front doors.

They make a couple more turns, then Joe tells them to stop.

His dad turns in his seat. "Where are we, son?"

Joe glances at the cheerful home, its clapboards painted a stormy blue with white trim. The paved walkway leading to the front door. The recently mowed lawn stretching across the front yard. He never had a yard when he was a kid, always had to play football at the local park. And never with his dad who had to work two jobs to keep meals on the table.

"This is your new home." Joe rests a hand on their shoulders.

His mom bursts into tears. His dad covers his chest with both hands, the color leaching from his face.

"It's too much," his mom says.

Joe ignores her. "Three bedrooms, two and a half baths,

living room, open plan kitchen and even an office. It has great light. I thought you could use it to paint, Mom." There is an easel and a canvas and a selection of acrylic paint waiting for her in that room.

His dad shakes his head. "I don't know how we can ever repay you."

Joe snakes his hand through the front seats and grabs his dad's hand. "You guys are the ones who invested in me. You put all your faith and money into that nanite pill. Now it's time to cash in."

Joe leaves his parents in their new home. It's already been furnished and there's no need to go back to their shitty apartment. He takes an Uber home. It's only ten minutes. And he chats with the driver the whole way. Once the driver realizes who Joe is, they talk ball. And Joe learns of the Californian player who recently got annihilated by the opposition. He's dead. Even though he was a bulk.

Bulks can still be injured or killed. Joe thinks of his own body, the genetic enhancements that made him who he is. The power, the strength, the speed—but also the risks, the unknowns.

CHAPTER 3

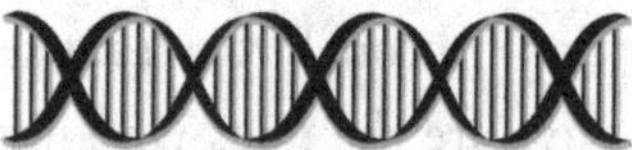

Six Months Later

THE ROAR of the crowd washes over him, sending a thrill down his spine.

"Ready to crush it out there?" his teammate, Mike, asks with a playful elbow to Joe's side.

Joe chuckles. "You know it. I might even let the other team get within ten yards of me this time."

As he surveys the field, Joe's mind wanders to the upcoming match. Since he took that pill, it's all come so easily. Almost too easily. Even though ninety-nine percent of pro ball players are also bulk, Joe dominates them all.

"Alright, Rucker! You're up!" Coach Harrison bellows from the sideline.

Joe jogs onto the field. He lines up, muscles coiled and ready. The ball snaps, and he's off like a shot, barreling along the field with impossible speed.

"Coming through!" he shouts, a laugh bubbling inside his chest as he dodges defenders.

He's almost at the end zone when he feels it—a sickening crunch in his knee as a defender dives low, catching him off guard. Joe stumbles, his momentum carrying him forward even as pain explodes through his leg.

Time seems to slow as he falls, the ground rushing up to meet him. *This can't be happening.*

He slams against the turf, his enhanced body absorbing most of the impact. But his knee—his knee is on fire. The world around Joe fades into a hazy blur, the roar of the crowd becoming a distant echo. He stares at the sky, the bright stadium lights piercing his eyes, casting everything in a surreal glow. The smell of freshly cut grass fills his nostrils, mixing with the coppery tang of blood and sweat.

He tries to move, to sit up, but his body won't cooperate. Every breath sends a fresh wave of agony radiating from his knee, as if a thousand needles are stabbing into the joint. He clenches his jaw, fighting back the scream that threatens to tear from his throat.

Gradually, the faces of his teammates come into focus above him. As he lies there, gasping, the realization hits him harder than any tackle: something is very, very wrong.

"Joe! Joe, can you hear me?" Coach's voice seems distant, muffled by the ringing in his ears.

Joe tries to respond, but all that comes out is a groan. He attempts to stand, but his leg gives way, sending a new wave of agony through him.

"Don't move, son," Coach says, his usual gruff demeanor softened by concern. "We're getting help."

As Joe lies there, staring at the sky, he can't help but think of all the dreams that might have just shattered along with his knee. This is his first season in the NFL. He can't afford time off for an injury he never thought would occur. He is just starting to make a name for himself—all of it seems to be slipping away like sand through his fingers.

"Hang in there," Mike says, kneeling beside him. "You'll be back on your feet in no time."

Joe manages a weak smile, but inside, a creeping dread begins to take hold. What if this is it? What if this is where his dream ends?

The world blurs into a kaleidoscope of colors and sounds as an ambulance screeches to a halt and two quick-footed medics arrive at his side with a stretcher. His team helps to lift his bulk onto the gurney.

"Easy does it," one medic says. "This guy's built like a tank."

Joe tries to laugh, but it comes out as a pained wheeze. "Guess I should've...gone for the agility nanites instead of bulk, huh?" His attempt at humor falls flat as another wave of pain washes over him.

The crowd's cheers fade into worried murmurs as he's wheeled towards the waiting ambulance. Joe catches glimpses of concerned faces in the stands, his teammates watching with a mix of shock and sympathy.

"You're gonna be okay, Rucker," Coach calls, jogging alongside the gurney. "We'll see you back on the field before you know it."

Joe wants to believe him, but the throbbing in his knee tells a different story. As they load him into the ambulance in strobes of blue, his mind goes blank. He can't think of the future, or of the past, but the present is an agonizing limbo.

The ride to the hospital is a blur of sirens and sharp turns. The pain is relentless. Each bump in the road sends fresh spikes of agony through his leg.

"How bad is it?" Joe pushes the question through his clenched teeth to the EMT monitoring his vitals.

The EMT's hesitation speaks volumes. "We'll know more once we get you to the hospital, but...it looks pretty serious."

Joe closes his eyes, fists his hands, tries not to cry. He can't remember the last time he cried. Okay, that's a lie. He cried when the NFL contract came through. Both him and his dad. *Dad. Mom.* He wants his parents. At nineteen years old, he wants his parents.

When they arrive at the hospital, Joe steels himself for what's to come. The gurney is wheeled through bustling corridors, fluorescent lights harsh against his eyes. He catches his reflection in a passing window and never wants to see it again. The haunted eyes speak of an uncertainty he thought he left behind.

"Hang in there," a nurse says kindly as they prepare him for examination. "We'll get you fixed up."

Joe nods, but inside his armored skin, shudders of anxiety streak through his limbs. As the doctors crowd around him, discussing his injury in hushed tones, Joe can't shake the feeling that this might be the end of everything he's worked for. A clipboard with an official-looking piece of paper is thrust in front of his face. Someone asks for his signature, which he scrawls across the page. An oxygen mask is placed over his face and he is wheeled into an operating room, the lights brightening by a gazillion kilowatts.

Joe's eyes roll back into his head, and then everything goes dark.

✕✕✕✕✕

Uncomfortable, Joe shifts on the bed, wincing as pain shoots through his knee. He takes in his surroundings. He's wearing a hospital gown and a thick bandage surrounds his knee. A familiar figure appears in the doorway and Joe's heart lifts.

"Coach," he says, managing a weak smile, the nerves in his face not fully powering after the heavy dose of anesthetic. "Good to see you."

Coach Harrison enters, his usual booming voice oddly subdued. "How you holding up, Rucker?"

Joe shrugs, his attempt at nonchalance betrayed by the strain in his voice. "Been better. I'm hoping the surgery worked a miracle. I know I'll be out for a while, but I promise I'll make it up to you."

Coach Harrison's face remains neutral. No sign of a tell. He takes a couple of steps closer to Joe's bed and hovers at the edge, hands shoved in his pockets. Now the tells are popping out all over the place.

Joe's stomach twists.

"Listen, kid," Coach begins, and Joe quashes the urge to squeeze his eyes closed and stick his fingers in his ears. "I've been talking with management about your options..."

Joe's attempts to sit up, but the small movement sends a shooting pain through his knee. "And?"

"Your contract...it doesn't cover regeneration nanites. Junior status and all that."

The words hit Joe like a tackle. He wondered why he was rushed into surgery. Regeneration nanites have been on the market for years, expensive, but common in most NFL contracts. "But...but I thought—"

"I know, I know," Harrison interjects. "Truth is, we've rarely needed them for younger players. Your age and enhancements were supposed to prevent this kind of thing. You've had one of the newer nanites. No one has incurred an injury this severe before. We didn't think it was possible."

How *was* it possible?

Joe thinks back to the tackle. To the bulk that slammed into him. The force of the impact shattered his kneecap, despite his armored skin. "I thought the surgery was supposed to help..."

Coach shakes his head. "Bulk skin. Can't be penetrated by knives or needles or scalpels. They tried..."

"There's gotta be something we can do, right? I mean, I can't just—"

A knock at the door interrupts them. Joe's agent, Tanya, steps in, her usual confident stride noticeably absent.

"Hey, superstar," she says, wearing a smile that doesn't reach her eyes.

Joe's heart rips in two. "Tanya, please tell me you've got good news."

She shakes her head, avoiding his gaze. "I'm sorry, Joe. The company...they're letting you go."

"What?" Joe's voice cracks. "But I just got started! One season and that's it?"

Tanya's words tumble out, rehearsed and hollow. "There's no point keeping an injured player on the books. And your reputation...it's not big enough yet for the speaker circuit or endorsements."

Joe's world crumbles around him. He stares at his hands, at the stupid pattern on the hospital gown, at the starkness of the starched sheets. None of this is real. It can't be. "So that's it? I'm just...*done?*"

An explosive silence fills the room. Joe swallows around the immovable lump in his throat, tastes ash in his mouth. He lays his head back on the pillow and feels like he's sinking through the mattress to a world he doesn't know.

Tanya places a tentative hand on his arm, but her touch is cool and unwelcome.

Joe shuts his eyes, listens to the sounds of his frustrated breathing. Pretends that his world, and his heart, aren't breaking apart.

Maybe he'll stay here forever. He sure as hell can't face his coach or agent again, let alone his teammates. And goddammit, his parents. They risked everything for this one opportunity, and he's blown it. All because he didn't read his contract thoroughly enough. Who even reads the fine print?

Joe shakes his head. That's no excuse. He listened to Tanya, signed on the dotted line when she said the deal was beyond competitive, didn't even think about the risk of injury. How can a bulk with armored skin get injured?

And yet...it happened.

Joe's gaze drifts to the window, the cityscape beyond a blur of neon and chrome. His thoughts race to the modest house on the outskirts of town, the one he'd proudly shown his parents just months ago. A lump forms in his throat as he remembers their beaming faces.

"At least I managed to do something good," he mutters, more to himself than anyone else.

Tanya's brow furrows. "What's that, Joe?"

He turns to her. "The house. Got my folks a place of their own. And a car that actually runs." His chuckle is hollow. "Guess I should be grateful for that, huh?"

But the momentary relief fades as quickly as it came. Joe's mind whirs with calculations—utility bills, his parents' medical expenses. The realization hits him like a freight train.

"God," he whispers, raking a hand through his hair. "What am I gonna do now? Football's all I know. It's why I..." He glances down at his massive frame, a reminder of the choice that led him here.

"There are other options," Tanya offers, but her tone lacks conviction.

Joe snorts. "Like what? Circus freak? Professional wall?"

"Joe," Coach Harrison interjects, his voice gruff but not unkind. "You're a smart kid. You'll figure something out."

But Joe barely hears him. His thoughts are a maelstrom of worry and regret. "I should've listened to Hal," he mutters.

"Hal Small?" Coach asks, surprised. "You know him?"

Joe nods absently. "Met him at a few games. He always said we were putting too much faith in these enhancements. Said there'd be a price to pay someday."

The irony of it all isn't lost on Joe. He' laughed off Hal's warnings, drunk on the promise of glory and riches. Now, as he sits here, broken and discarded, those words haunt him.

"I just…I don't know what comes next," Joe says, his voice small despite his imposing stature. "How do I tell my folks? How do I make this right?"

The silence that follows is heavy with unspoken fears and shattered dreams. Neither Coach nor his agent can help. He's on his own.

CHAPTER 4

Joe grits his teeth, forcing himself through the series of exercises in the gym. The throbbing ache in his knee screams with every movement. Each session is a grueling war of torturous stretches that threaten to snap his already weakened muscles, relentless exercises that push him to the brink of exhaustion, and the incessant beep and whirr of machines that mock his efforts. He's been doing this for three agonizing months. They made him a cake when he was able to walk unaided, but unless Joe can get back to a field, it doesn't seem like such a big step to him.

He *will* play again.

He tells himself this every day, but the voice that started shouting it is now only a whisper.

"Take it easy," the physio says with a wry smile, handing him a towel. "You're making the rest of us look bad."

Joe smirks as he performs another squat, ignoring the dull ache of pain radiating from his knee.

The therapist chuckles. "You're really pushing yourself today, Joe."

"Got no choice," Joe replies, shaking out his leg.

"You've been making great progress."

"Gotta get back to the game before they forget who I am," he says, wincing against the hollowness of his words.

With each passing day, he can feel himself walking steadier, the limp less pronounced, but unless he can return to his previous peak physical fitness, no team is going to take a chance on him.

"Don't forget to continue your exercises while you're in Central City," the therapist tells him.

He throws her a mock salute. "Absolutely."

"And good luck," she says, her face turning serious. "Your case is the first one of its kind. I hope it sets a precedent for the future."

Joe never intended to get into politics, to become a lobbyist, or have anything to do with the NFL administration. But he wants to fight for what's fair. The bulk nanite has only been around a couple of decades. Teething problems are still being worked out. A full document of weaknesses hasn't yet been calculated. And so it's only right that sports contracts should protect their players. But that's a side dream. As selfish as it sounds, his priority is to play ball again. And he'll damn well fight like a hellcat for the opportunity, even if he has to take on the President himself.

A few buses, a couple of trains, a cab, and most of a week later, Joe arrives in Central City, the rolling wheat fields of Kansas a distant memory. He is dwarfed by its skyscrapers that pierce the heavens, their steel and glass facades reflecting the punishing sun. It's a world away from the open fields and starry nights of his hometown.

"Here goes nothing," he mutters to himself, stepping into the NFL administration building. Plaques and trophies line the lobby, each one representing the triumphs and glories of past football legends. Photographs cover the walls, capturing pivotal moments in the sport's history, while the floor is polished to a gleaming shine. The irony isn't lost on him. Here he is, a fallen rookie, seeking a scientific miracle.

Wood polish and freshly cut grass tinge the air, reminiscent of football fields and training camps. He doesn't know how they managed that, probably some kind of scent nanite. If they can afford to spend so wastefully on their décor, surely they can offer him a regeneration pill. A spark of hope unfurls in his chest.

"Sir, how can we help you today?" the receptionist asks, her gaze drifting to meet his eyes.

"Joe Rucker," he begins, a rehearsed pitch at the ready. "I'm here for my appointment to request a regeneration nanite. I've been told it's my best shot at...well, at getting back what I lost."

"Please take a seat, Mr. Rucker," she replies with a practiced smile, gesturing toward the waiting area. "Someone will be with you shortly."

The taste of anticipation and nerves hang on Joe's tongue as he prepares himself for the meeting ahead. He settles into a chair that's too small for his bulk and a sudden laugh bursts from him, raising eyebrows from a few of the milling people in the lobby.

Half an hour later, Joe is called through to a meeting

room where ten people in expensive suits are gathered round a polished, oak conference table, fingers poised over laptops, all eyeing him with stern expressions.

He swallows. Nerves never got the better of him on the field and he's sure as hell not going to let them get the better of him now. After straightening his tie, he goes around the table and shakes everyone's hands, even if it uses a couple minutes of his allotted time. He plans to leave an impression. A favorable one.

He takes a gulp of the offered water and then launches into his memorized speech, appealing to their better natures, mentioning lack of documented bulk attributes, citing other injured players and contract loopholes. Their expression doesn't change, and Joe ignores the clenching of his stomach. When he is done, they carry on making their notes for a moment.

A man in a blue pinstripe suit stands and offers his hand. "Thank you, Mr. Rucker. We'll be in touch."

That's it?

Why can't they decide now?

Surely, it's a no-brainer?

He is escorted back into the lobby and left to twist in the metaphorical wind.

Clenching his teeth, he leaves the building and makes his way to Hal's place. He could use a stiff drink and an ear. Maybe a punch bag or two.

A half hour later, Joe presses the doorbell of a modest row house. Hal, with his stocky build and a face that tells tales of gridiron glory, extends a hand and a genuine smile.

"Welcome, buddy," Hal says, the warmth in his voice taking away the edge of homesickness.

"Thanks for having me, Hal."

In the corner, an unadjusted toddler with curly brown hair like his father's teeters over, eyeing Joe with open curiosity. His wife, a petite woman with a welcoming face, offers Joe a tentative smile as she sweeps their child into her arms.

"Joe, meet Brandon and Mara," Hal introduces them, nodding first to his son, then his wife. "Guys, this is Joe."

"Nice to meet you both," Joe says, crouching to be at eye level with Brandon, who hides his face in his mother's neck. Mara smiles and touches his arm, a maternal pressure that fills Joe with relief.

"Sorry about the mess," Mara says, gesturing to the scattered toys and crayon drawings that adorn the living room floor.

Joe waves away the apology. "Looks lived in. It's nice."

Hal leads Joe to the kitchen where they share a beer. The conversation turns from small talk about the journey to Central City and Joe's dubious hopes, to a subject that surprises the hell out of him.

"Have you heard about the resistance?" Hal asks, lowering his voice as if the walls can hear.

"Resistance?" Joe frowns, running his fingers down the cold glass of his beer bottle. "Against what?"

"Genetic enhancements," Hal replies. "There's a growing number of people who are against it all—the pills, the nanites, the classist system it's created."

Joe leans back, absorbing the news. It's a sharp departure

from the physiotherapy room's sterile optimism, where technology was the savior. Nanites are meant to aid, to cure, to abolish disease. And yes, he'll admit, it's gone way beyond that. Enhancements. But if he hadn't taken the bulk pill, he'd never have seen an NFL contract. There must be other people like him, given a nanite, experienced an injury or negative side effect and then thrown to the wilds to cope on their own. Back in Kansas, where he is surrounded mostly by other players, he's never heard a negative word against enhancements. But being in the city, he can see how Hal would have heard mutterings.

"They say something is coming," Hal says. "Some kind of mandate from President Bear. And the unadjusteds are getting ready to act. A resistance. Rebellion. An uprising. It's run by this teacher, an ex-karate champion, and some teenager called Matt Lawson."

"Never thought I'd see the day," Joe says, his thoughts racing. He pictures his parents, unadjusted and vulnerable in Kansas, far from the turmoil of Central City but perhaps not safe from its reach.

"Are they...do they have much support?" Joe asks, trying to gauge the size of the wave that could crash over society.

"More every day," Hal whispers, running a hand through his short, dark hair. "People are waking up to the fact that not everyone can afford to be *better*. That being human shouldn't come with a price tag."

Joe nods. Once, he would have dismissed such talk as fear of progress. Now, with the weight of his injury and dashed dreams bearing down on him, he's not so sure.

"Excuse me one sec," Joe says, pulling out his phone. He steps into the hallway and dials a familiar number. The phone rings, each tone stretching longer than the last until finally, his mother picks up.

"Mom? It's Joe. Just wanted to check in, make sure you and Dad are alright."

"Joe! We're fine, just the usual around here. But how are you? Did you get to Central City okay?"

"Yeah, Mom, I'm good. Staying with a friend." Joe glances back toward the kitchen, where Hal is grabbing a couple more beers from the fridge. "Listen, there's talk going around about a resistance against the enhancements. You guys keep your ears open, alright? Stay safe."

"Of course, honey. We always do. You don't need to worry about us, you take care of yourself."

"Will do, Mom. Love you."

"Love you too."

Joe hangs up, concern lingering like the ache in his knee. He returns to the kitchen, finding Hal and Mara deep in hushed conversation.

"Everything alright back home?" Hal asks.

"Seems to be," Joe replies. "For now, anyway."

"Good," Hal says firmly, pushing the fresh beer into Joe's hand. "That's good."

As Joe takes his seat, joining the quiet solidarity at the table, he can't help but wonder what the outcome will be—not just for himself, but for everyone caught in the crosshairs of a world divided by DNA. This is so much bigger than one regeneration pill.

Joe shuffles into the tribunal chamber, his knee issuing a small protest with each step. The room is as sterile as the future it governs—steel gray walls, a lonely clock ticking out the seconds, and a long table where three adjudicators sit like modern-day deities.

"State your case," the middle adjudicator commands, her voice crisp in the silence.

Joe frowns. "I did that last week when I met with—"

"You need to restate your case for the official documented process."

Joe's heart flutters. With a deep breath that does little to steady his nerves, he begins. "I'm here to request access to a regeneration nanite. Without it, my career—" he swallows, "—my life, as I know it, is over."

"Proceed with the evidence," another adjudicator, a man with a scanner for eyes, says.

The days that follow are a blur of testimonials, medical reports, and Joe's own heartfelt pleas. He watches as his shadow dances on the wall behind him, a distorted echo of the athlete he used to be. The adjudicators listen, or seem to, as impassive as the technology they control.

Finally, after what feels like an eternity compressed into days, the verdict comes down like a hammer. "Joseph Rucker, your appeal for a regeneration nanite is hereby dismissed."

"Please," Joe tries, "without it, I can't—"

"Next case," the woman interrupts, not unkindly, but firmly enough to close the door on further argument.

Stunned, Joe exits the chamber, his limp more pronounced. He steps onto the crowded streets of Central City, where holographic ads promise perfection with every pill swallowed. No one looks up from their screens, no one offers kind words, no one cares.

"Hey, aren't you Joe Rucker? The rookie who scored that impossible touchdown?"

Joe turns to find a kid, no older than twelve, looking up at him with wide eyes. There's something pure in that gaze, untouched by Joe's newly adopted cynicism.

"That was me," Joe admits with a half-smile, trying to keep the bitterness at bay. "Before the injury."

"Man, that game was insane! Sorry about your leg, though," the kid says, staring at his knee.

"Thanks, kid." Joe claps him on the shoulder.

"Good luck, Mr. Rucker," the kid calls as he disappears into the throng, leaving Joe alone with the ghost of his past triumphs.

For a moment, Joe stands still amidst the flow of people, the towering buildings reflecting the evening sun. It's a beautiful, cruel city that doesn't pause for anyone, not even for an eight-foot former football star. But then again, Joe Rucker isn't one to stand idle for long, even if it's on a bad knee.

He hobbles along the neon-lit sidewalk, the glow from the advertisements casting surreal shadows on his path. The city's pulse throbs in his ears, a discordant rhythm that compels him to return to the wheat fields of his home.

He ducks into an alley, away from the prying eyes and the ever-present screens, needing a moment where the world isn't watching him fall apart. The cool brick wall feels rough against his back as he slides to the ground.

"Okay, Joe," he mutters to himself, "where do you go from here?" His voice echoes off the walls, mocking him with its emptiness. He's always been the guy with a plan, but now the playbook's been torn to shreds, and there's no coach to call in a new strategy.

"Guess I'm officially a has-been at nineteen." They have pills to change DNA, to turn mortals into gods, but none to mend a broken spirit.

He fishes out his phone. No missed calls, no messages. Silence is the cruelest sound when you're looking for a lifeline.

"Mom and Dad bet everything on me," he whispers, the screen's light making him blink. "And I dropped the ball. Literally." Pride had swelled in their faces when they saw him bulked up, their savings turned into muscle and might. Now, debt and disappointment are all he has to offer them.

Using the wall for support, he stands. There's no nanite pill to give him a second chance, no miracle cure for a derailed destiny. Joe Rucker, once destined for greatness, is now just another face in the crowd.

CHAPTER 5

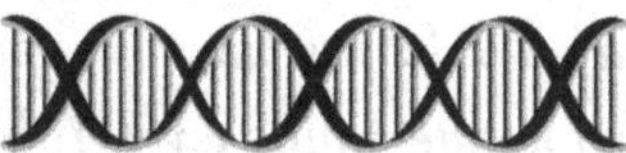

JOE EYES the gathering as he limps down the street, his hair buried under a cap and the personalized billboards advising him to buy a sunblock nanite. As he approaches the growing mass of people, the crowd thickens until it's five people deep outside a tech store. An unusual tension lines their faces, so he pauses to see what they're all looking at. On each of the several screens displayed in the front window, President's Bear's face looms across the entire width. Curiosity locks him in place. Curiosity, and a hint of fear.

"This is a national announcement. All unadjusteds age twelve and over will now be required to take a nanite pill to enhance their abilities. With threats and competition from overseas, we must do more to further the strength of our country." The president's red eyes emanate ruthless determination.

Required to take a nanite? Well, Joe's already taken one, and look where that got him. Is President Bear going to personally foot the bill for regeneration nanites when it all hits the fan? Unlikely.

On screen, the president continues. "*The nanite representative agency is on its way to every school right now. They will assign each eligible unadjusted a ticket number. You are not permitted to leave before you have your ticket. This ticket will tell you which day within the next two weeks you will be assessed for an appropriate nanite level. You'll notice many of those assessments start today...*"

This is some jacked-up vison of a mutated future. Is he living in a sci-fi novel? How the hell can the president take away people's rights? Joe catches eyes with a few in the crowd. Some are triumphant and pumping arms. A couple are fearful and back away from the gathering.

"*Once this assessment is complete, we will proceed to residences to evaluate the unadjusted adults. I expect each unadjusted individual to join the strength of the adjusted superbeings. Failure to comply will result in unfortunate circumstances.*"

Unfortunate circumstances? What the hell does that mean? Joe's hands ball into fists at his sides. This is wrong. His parents, his friends, everyone he cares about—they deserve better than to be reduced to cogs in President Bear's twisted machine. But what can he do against the full might of the government?

"*Our country is the most powerful in the world. Your loyalty and patriotism are expected. But in case you need a reminder of what happens to traitors...*"

The image on the screen shifts abruptly, replacing President Bear's contemptuous face with a scene from two years prior. Joe's heart constricts as he recognizes the woman on the screen: Dr. Margaret Melody, her wrists bound in front of her as she's dragged forward by a pair of heavily armed soldiers.

Joe remembers the day Dr. Melody was arrested, remembers the shock and disbelief that rippled through the country. She was one of the lead scientists on the nanite program, had worked tirelessly to develop the technology that promised to cure disease and regenerate lost limbs. But when the program took a turn, when the focus shifted from healing to enhancing, Dr. Melody spoke out against it.

On the screen, soldiers shove her to her knees, their weapons trained on her head. Dr. Melody lifts her chin defiantly, her eyes blazing with a fierce determination even as tears stream down her cheeks.

"I will not be silenced," she declares, her voice ringing out clear and strong. *"I will not stand by and watch as our humanity is stripped away, as we become nothing more than puppets dancing to the tune of those in power. I will fight, with every breath in my body, to protect the unadjusted, to preserve our right to choose our own destiny."*

The screen reverts to President Bear. Joe barely hears his final remarks over the blood pounding in his ears. His parents. They're still in Kansas, unaware that their worst fears are coming true. He has to get to them, somehow, before the nanite reps do.

Around him, the street erupts into chaos. Shouts and screams fill the air as the unadjusteds panic, bolting in all directions like players scrambling after a loose ball. The altereds—those already enhanced—seem to feed off the fear, their eyes taking on a feral, predatory gleam. But not Joe. He senses violence in the air and trepidation sends tension lancing down his spine.

Joe is jostled from all sides as people push past him. A scuffle breaks out nearby, a winged altered versus an unadjusted. The altered moves inhumanly fast, appearing behind the other man and seizing him in a chokehold. The unadjusted claws at his attacker's grip, feet kicking fruitlessly.

Ducking his head, Joe plunges into the frantic crowd. He has to keep moving. Get off the streets, get somewhere safe to regroup and plan his next steps. He won't let them take his parents, or their freedom. Not without a fight. If he can get to them.

Joe weaves through the throng, his bulk frame an advantage as he shoulders past grasping hands and desperate faces. His knee aches, but he doesn't have time to nurse it now.

A piercing scream rips through the air. Joe whirls around to see a young woman cowering against a building, her arms raised in a futile attempt to shield herself from the threatening figure of an altered. The man's eyes blaze with a feral intensity, his muscles bulging grotesquely beneath his skin as he raises a clawed hand to strike.

Without hesitation, Joe lunges, his enhanced reflexes propelling him forward. He reaches the altered just as the man's talons whistle through the air, catching his wrist in an iron grip. The altered snarls, his face contorting with rage, but Joe holds firm, his own strength more than a match for the other man's.

"Leave her alone," Joe growls. "Walk away now, and no one has to get hurt."

The altered hesitates, his gaze flickering between Joe and the terrified woman. For a moment, it seems as if he might back down. But then, with a roar of fury, he wrenches his arm free and lunges at Joe, his fingers curled into claws.

Joe reacts instinctively, dropping to one knee—his good one—and sweeping the altered's legs out from under him. The man crashes to the ground, but he's up again in an instant, his eyes burning with murderous intent. All around them, more altereds are emerging from the chaos, their faces twisted with a feral hunger as they zero in on the fleeing unadjusteds. The crowd swallows both the man and the unadjusted woman and Joe is left standing in the middle of the streaming masses.

He elbows his way through to a quieter street, pushing his knee more than he should, but he has no choice. With narrowed focus, he keeps running until he finds himself alone. A flash of movement catches his eye and he flinches, but it's just his own reflection in a darkened store window. Eight feet of muscle and armored skin, features he once took pride in. Now they feel more like a curse, marking him as something other than human. He doesn't want to end up on the wrong side of whatever is about to go down.

His phone buzzes insistently against his thigh and he fumbles it out, hoping against hope it's his parents. Instead, a message from Hal glows on the screen.

Hideout for the unadjusteds. Sending coordinates. Meet you there.

Joe forwards the coordinates to his parents, knowing it's too far for them to travel without getting caught, but he has to try something.

He imagines his parents herded like cattle, their fate decided by a cold, uncaring system. It will take him five days to travel back to Kansas, longer now that the mandate has been issued. The country is in lockdown, the borders sealed tight. Traveling back to Kansas is a suicide mission, a futile attempt that would likely end with him in a cell right alongside his parents. Whatever is going to happen to them will have happened before he can get there.

Joe makes an abrupt turn and runs in the other direction, following the directions on his phone, back through the crowds. He'll get to the cave, regroup, then figure out how to get to his parents.

The street blurs past, graffitied walls and shuttered windows, as Joe races toward an uncertain fate, heart hammering in time with his thundering steps. The power thrumming through his body, once a source of pride and purpose, now feels like a mockery. What good is being a bulk if he can't protect the people he loves?

The street around him buzzes with tension, unadjusted citizens hurrying past with hunched shoulders and darting eyes. But even as he walks, his mind races with questions. How organized is the resistance? Do they have weapons? Do they have plans beyond escaping? How long can they hold out against the might of the government?

He shakes his head, banishing the dark thoughts. He'll get to the cave and then worry about the next steps.

A group of altered teens shove past him, their laughter harsh and mocking. Joe grits his teeth, fighting the urge to confront them. He knows it's not their fault, not really. The nanites have changed them, warped their perceptions and dulled their empathy. But it's hard not to resent them, these privileged few who have never known the struggle of being unaltered. Don't they remember their time before?

As he walks, Joe's hand drifts to his pocket, feeling the outline of his phone. He thumbs his parents' number.

We're sorry, but the number you have dialed is no longer in service. The individuals associated with this number have been relocated to a secure facility for their own protection. Please direct any further inquiries to the Office of Adjusted Affairs. Thank you for your cooperation.

Joe's blood runs cold, his fingers tightening around the phone until the plastic creaks in protest. *A secure facility.* They've taken them. President Bear has taken his parents.

Joe clenches his jaw, forcing himself to focus on the task at hand. He can't help his parents if he gets himself killed on the streets.

With a final, regretful glance at the growing pandemonium surrounding him, Joe increases his speed, his long strides eating up the pavement as he races towards the one place he knows he might find allies.

The resistance is waiting. And Joe is ready to join their ranks.

The hideout Hal mentioned is through the forest. It will take him a few days to hike there, and he's going to need supplies.

The streets grow quieter as he moves away from the city center. He makes a quick stop at Hal's place to find it deserted. There are signs of a scuffle: a broken coffee table, a turned over chair, a carton of milk spilled on the kitchen tiles. Trying not to give in to panic, he grabs his stuff and shoves it into a rucksack. Remembers a water flask at the last minute, then heads out the door. He catches sight of soldiers marching through the streets, but they pay him no mind, his bulk status is a free pass. No one will think to question him with his enhancements being so openly physical.

A report of automatic gunfire sounds, startling him and making him wince. He doesn't look over his shoulder. He doesn't want to see what happened. Instead, despite the circumstances, an inkling of hope ignites. He might not be able to play ball anymore, but being a bulk brings other opportunities. He can help the unadjusteds. His strength, his reflexes, his speed...it can all help the unadjusteds. Because they're going to have to fight against an army of people just like him.

Finally, he reaches the edge of the city, the forest looming ahead. Joe takes a deep breath, squaring his shoulders. Whatever happens next, he knows he's not alone. There are others like him, others who refuse to be cowed by President Bear's tyranny. Together, they will find a way to resist, to fight back, to reclaim their humanity in a world determined to strip it away.

With a final glance over his shoulder, Joe steps into the woods. Dr. Melody's words echo in his mind, her fierce determination and unwavering courage giving him strength.

CHAPTER 6

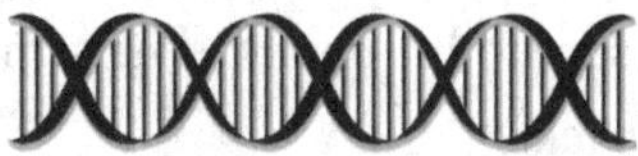

Joe trudges through the dense underbrush, stooping beneath low-hanging branches and trampling over ferns. Sweat trickles down his brow as he pushes aside a tangle of vines, revealing a rusted machete half-buried in the soil.

"Well, hello there," he says with a grin, prying the blade from the earth. "Looks like you could use a good home."

He turns the machete over in his hands, admiring the weight of it. The metal is pitted but solid, the wooden handle worn smooth by use. With a few passes across his pant leg, Joe wipes away the grime.

As he slips the machete into his belt, his thoughts drift to his family back in Kansas. All he knows is that they're in a compound. He ditched his phone a couple hours ago when he couldn't get any signal. With no phone, no one can track him. But lack of connectivity means he has zero information about their whereabouts, or if they're...alive or dead. Last information he received was about the merciless gunning down of unadjusteds in the streets when they refused to comply.

President Bear and the Nanite Enforcement Agency are about as serious as a heart attack, and he's pretty sure they'll be using tracking tech and spyware to round up any rogue individuals. Even if he is a bulk. He is still ignoring the ticket number that was sent to his phone. The same cell buried in a bush a few miles back.

If he can believe the message he received when he tried to contact his parents, they're in a compound. Where? He has no idea. But hopefully it means they're safe. If they comply, they'll get food and water. Won't they? They can't starve them. President Bear needs the unadjusteds. Joe witnessed firsthand how the altereds all went nuts as soon as the unadjusteds started running. He's not a scientist. Wasn't his strongest subject during high school and so he has no way to explain it. Seeing it was enough, though, all that murderous intent in their eyes. That guy who attacked the unadjusted woman in the alley. And even a bulk can die if another altered is serious enough about putting him down. Better he's alone. In the woods. Where he has nothing to think about but the outside world. The safety of his parents. And what the hell is going to happen next.

Joe shakes his head, pushing away the difficult emotions. At least with the machete he can hunt. Not that he's tried it before, not for years, but he's willing to give it a go. And hell, he doesn't have much choice. Berries and bark won't satisfy his increased metabolism.

He scans the surrounding trees, searching for a branch to fashion into a spear. With the machete, his memories of growing up hunting with his grandpa, and his own two hands, he'll learn to fend for himself.

Joe's grip tightens on the machete as he forges ahead, determination his overriding emotion as he strides beneath the leafy canopy. He follows a babbling stream for a couple days, hiking into the heart of the forest. His enhanced hearing detects every rustle of leaves, every chirp and chitter of the surrounding wildlife. But as he bends to refill his canteen, a new sound reaches his ears: the distant thrum of helicopter blades slicing through the air.

Frowning, Joe straightens. He cocks his head, listening intently. There it is again, growing louder by the second. And beneath it, the unmistakable crunch of boots on fallen branches. Soldiers?

He catches sight of a blur of heavy boots. Shouts in the distance. He backs into a shrub, sinks to his knees into the soil, even though it sends a slice of pain through the injured one. What are they looking for?

A flicker of unease passes through him, but Joe shrugs it off. With his bulk appearance, he's sure he can talk his way out of any situation. He's clearly an altered and no one can question that. They might give him a slap on the wrist for not following official procedure, but surely that will be the worst of it.

Still, he can't help wonder who they're looking for out here in the middle of nowhere. Joe hasn't come across a single soul since he entered the woods, so it's not like there's a whole bunch of unadjusteds trampling through the forest. They must be after someone in particular. Someone high profile. The thoughts irritate the back of Joe's neck and send a creeping dread skittering down his spine. If he comes across an unadjusted in need, he'll do what he can to help. Hell, it's the least he can do. If he can't help his parents, he's damn well going to help anyone else he comes across. This is where his fight starts.

Lost in his thoughts, he almost walks straight into the soldier. He stops abruptly as their gazes collide. The soldier is shorter than him, muscular, but not a bulk. Joe heaves an internal sigh of relief. If it comes to it, Joe can take him.

The soldier swings his automatic weapon in Joe's direction and Joe thrusts his hands skyward.

"Who are you and what are you doing in the woods?"

Joe searches his mind for a believable lie. He's never been the best at it, so he's going to have to channel his elementary school drama lessons. Which he sucked at.

"What's going on?" Joe asks, fighting the fear in his voice. "I've been camping for a few days...is this place off limits, or something?"

"Or something." The soldier smirks, then frowns, his eyes roaming Joe's small pack. "You on the run?"

Joe keeps his expression neutral. "From what? I'm just hear for a little piece and quiet."

"You haven't heard the announcement?"

"What announcement?"

"Where's your phone?"

Joe shakes his head. "No signal in the woods. Didn't bring it."

"How long have you been out here?"

"A few days."

The soldier takes that in.

"Is there a problem?" Joe asks, daring to lower his hands.

"Best you get yourself back to the city. Nanite enforcement program has been announced. You'll need to present yourself. Seeing as you're a bulk, it shouldn't be too arduous a process."

Joe gapes at him like it's the first time he's heard the news.

Lowering his gun, the soldier lets out a chuckle. "About time those unadjusteds finally upped their game."

"Right?" Joe plays along, but he has to clench the anger between his teeth. "Who are you looking for?"

"That's classified."

Joe shrugs, sweeps a hand around the woods. "Who am I going to tell?"

The soldier's eyes glint, readying to share juicy gossip. "You know that nanite scientist? Dr Melody? He fled with his daughter. A shit ton of unadjusteds ran after the announcement. Seems the altereds are struggling without the presence of the unadjusteds. Some kind of murder spree. President Bear wants him back. Wants him to fix it."

"Wow, that's...holy shit..."

"I know, right?"

"He even put a price on their heads. A million each. Alive. If you see them, that reward money could be yours, buddy."

I'm not your freaking buddy.

The anger and frustration overwhelm Joe. The worry over his parents. And now this witch hunt for a scientist and his teenaged daughter. Before the soldier can react, Joe whips out a hand and yanks the rifle from his grip. The soldier opens his mouth to shout, but Joe drops the rifle on the ground and covers the soldier's mouth with his hand. Before he can think too much about it, and knowing he has no choice, he snaps the soldier's neck. Quick and clean.

The soldier crumples at his feet, unseeing eyes staring up at him.

Joe has never taken a life. Never thought he would. It doesn't feel as bad as he thought it would. What the hell does that say about him?

He's officially joined the ranks of the resistance, that's what it says. Because that fight will not be without death.

Crouching, Joe switches off the soldier's radio, then wrestles his pack out from under him. He's got a couple changes of clothes inside, first aid supplies, and food. That will keep him going for a while. He shoves all his stuff into the larger pack, covers the soldier with a few branches, and turns his back on the whole regretful affair.

It's soldiers like that who rounded up his parents. Who gunned down unadjusteds in the street. Who would kill him if they knew which side he's on. And taking out one soldier is barely a dent in the resistance, but Joe is glad to be on the side of humanity. Even if it is ugly.

It's only going to get uglier.

He doesn't take the rifle. He buries it in the soil. Ever since his grandpa taught him to shoot, he's hated guns. The way it can end a life in a single blink. He'll have to face weapons at some point, but not now. *Not yet.* He feels more in control with the machete strapped to his belt.

As the sun dips lower in the sky, painting the clouds in shades of orange and pink, Joe makes camp in a small clearing sheltered by a towering oak. He finds a roll mat tied to the soldier's pack and uncurls it on the mossy ground. The scent of rich soil surrounds him as he settles in for the night, and one by one, stars wink into view.

Leaning back against the tree trunk, Joe tilts his face upward, drinking in the sight of the night sky. Out here, far from the light pollution of the cities, with only the nocturnal animals disturbing the quiet, Joe can almost believe the world hasn't gone to hell. And then, of course, there are the flash-backs from killing the soldier. Guilt twists his stomach. He didn't have to kill him, could have just walked away, but if the doc and his daughter truly are in the woods, perhaps taking out a soldier has helped them in some small way. He doesn't want to see them caught. And he hopes someone will have done the same for his parents.

Joe's eyes drift shut, but he can't stop thinking about the soldier, about how many others might be in the woods. The Melodys need help, but Joe can't take out President Bear's army on his own.

With a sigh, he rolls onto his side, trying to push the unease away. His knee needs a break, as well as the rest of his body.

The sharp snap of a twig jerks Joe from his dreamless sleep. His eyes fly open, every muscle tensing as he scans the darkness, searching for the source of the sound. The forest is unnaturally silent, the usual nighttime chorus of insects and nocturnal creatures conspicuously absent.

Another crack, closer this time. Joe scrambles to his feet, his heart pounding against his ribs. He reaches for the machete at his side, the cool wood of the handle offering a small measure of comfort.

And then he sees it.

A pair of glowing eyes gleaming in the shadows like smoldering embers. The creature steps into a shaft of moonlight, and Joe's breath catches in his throat. It's a dog, but unlike any he's seen before. Easily the size of a bear, with a coat as black as pitch and muscles rippling beneath its skin. Its muzzle is drawn back in a snarl, revealing rows of gleaming, razor-sharp teeth. It's not a dog. It's a *hellhound*.

"Easy there, buddy," Joe says softly, holding out his free hand in a placating gesture. "I don't want any trouble."

The hellhound growls, low and menacing, and begins to circle, its eyes never leaving Joe's face. He tightens his grip on the machete, his mind racing as he tries to remember everything he's ever learned about facing off against wild animals. Which is absolutely nothing. Hunting lessons with his grandpa were focused on him being the predator, not the prey.

He has armored skin. The hound shouldn't be able to hurt him, but it doesn't stop the fear coursing through Joe's limbs. There are four weak spots in a bulk. Each the size of a quarter. Big enough for a knife, or a bullet, or a claw, or a tooth to penetrate. Nape of the neck. Throat. Back of both knees. Bulks need medical treatment. With unpierceable skin, these small areas are necessary. And it's why his knee was injured.

Joe feels all four of the points tingle as the hound lunges, a blur of teeth and claws and fury. Joe reacts on instinct, his enhanced reflexes taking over as he sidesteps the attack and slices the machete down in a glittering arc.

The blade bites into the hellhound's shoulder, eliciting a

yelp of pain and rage. It whirls, its jaws snapping inches from Joe's face. He stumbles back, his foot catching on a root, and goes down hard, the machete flying from his grip.

The hellhound is on him in an instant, its hot breath ghosting over his skin as it lunges for his throat. Joe throws his hands up, catching the beast's jaws and straining to hold it at bay. Saliva drips onto his face as he struggles, his enhanced strength the only thing keeping those terrible teeth from eviscerating him.

With a roar of effort, Joe surges upward, throwing the hellhound off him. It tumbles away, but is back on its feet in an instant, poised to attack again. Joe lunches for the blade, but the dog—beast—hellhound is about to spring.

The jaws snap, bringing closer the reek of death and disease and everything he never wants to smell again. Joe circles his hands around the animal's neck, feels the muscles bulging under his grip, thinks he might not be as strong as he thought he was as the hound's teeth scrape against his cheek.

Fur against his chest. Saliva pooling onto his throat. Joe wrestles free from beneath the hound, keeping his hands tight around the neck even though the animal is bucking and jerking and snarling.

Joe gets his weight on top of the oversized excuse for a dog and pins him to the soil. Squeezes his hands. Squeezing, tighter, tighter, tighter...

Finally, the hound goes limp in his grip and Joe releases a shuddering breath.

For a long moment, Joe simply lies there, his chest heaving as he stares at the dead creature. "What the hell was that thing?" he whispers, his voice trembling.

Gingerly, he shoves the carcass aside and clambers to his feet, wincing at the ache in his knee. He retrieves the machete, his eyes darting nervously between the shadows, suddenly all too aware of how vulnerable he is out here.

If there are more of these things out here, engineered to hunt and kill, then he's in more danger than he imagined. And so are the Melodys.

CHAPTER 7

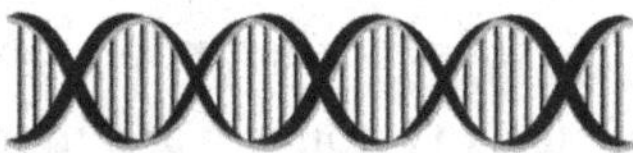

JOE CREEPS through the shadowy forest, his heavy footfalls crunching over twigs and leaves. The rhythmic whir of helicopter blades beat overhead, echoing through the trees. Beams of light slash through the sky high overhead. Joe grips the machete. He braces himself, muscles tense and ready.

Another hellhound could be lurking anywhere, waiting to pounce from the shadows with gnashing fangs. His last encounter was one he does not want to repeat.

After a few minutes, the sound of the helicopter fades.

His stomach grumbles, a hollow ache. How long has it been since his last full meal? He can't remember. He spots a flicker of movement ahead—a fat gray squirrel perched on a low branch.

Joe unslings his pack and rummages for some spare wire he found in the soldier's bag. Without making a sound, he fashions a snare. He sets the trap and retreats behind a tree to wait. Minutes tick by. The squirrel scampers down.

SNAP!

A clean catch. Joe grins. His grandpa would be proud. "Guess it's squirrel flambé for dinner tonight. Bon appétit!" He holds up the twitching carcass. "Sorry little dude, but a guy's gotta eat."

Joe builds a fire in the hollow of a trunk, hoping the sheer size of it and the thickness of the undergrowth will mask the flames and smoke. He can't stomach any more berries.

Remembering summers on his grandpa's farm, he skins and spits the squirrel, letting it roast over the crackling flames. Savory aromas waft into his nose, making his mouth water.

As meat sizzles, Joe allows himself a few minutes of rest, propping himself against a sturdy trunk. Stars wink through the full branches overhead. He looks at his hands. Hands capable of snapping necks and strangling hellhounds. Is that what his life is now? When his mind wanders to his parents, he shakes the thoughts away. The only way fear and stress won't overwhelm him is by staying in the moment.

He rotates the spit, his fire-retardant fingers useful for once. The squirrel looks about done, not that he's ever roasted a squirrel before, but he's too hungry to wait any longer. Joe tears into the meat, savoring each smoky morsel.

With grease running down his chin, he lets out a sigh, feeling a small measure of contentment. For the first time since stepping into the forest, Joe falls into a dreamless sleep. He wakes with the rising sun and animals scurrying through the underbrush. Yawns. Stretches. Latches onto the coordinates in his mind. He hopes he memorized them correctly. Numbers have never been his strength. Feels like he should be there by now. Although he has a keen sense of direction, he has no compass to prove he's traveling the right way. All he can do is keep on going.

Joe gathers his stuff and weaves between the trees, the machete swinging from his hand. A little over an hour later, a scream shatters the forest's eerie calm. Adrenaline surging, Joe pivots in a circle, looking for a threat. Another shriek sounds, followed by snarls and a man's agonized shout.

Joe charges toward the commotion, dodging branches that snag at his clothes. He bursts into a small clearing and freezes, taking in the grisly scene.

A behemoth hellhound, its matted fur slick with blood, lies twitching on the ground. A few feet away, a man writhes in pain, his leg bent at a sickening angle, crimson pooling beneath him. Beside the man, a girl retches violently, a bloodied knife trembling in her grip.

As Joe steps forward, the girl's head snaps up. Silver eyes, wide with terror and tears, lock onto his. She's pale, shaking like a leaf, but beneath the fear, there's a fierce determination in her eyes. She's a fighter, this one.

Helicopter blades whir overhead. The girl curses, fumbling for her pack. "Dad, stay with me," she pleads, voice cracking. "You have to take these."

She removes a bottle, shakes two pills into her palm. Nanites. With gentle hands, she coaxes them into the man's mouth even though he's hardly conscious.

Joe's heart clenches. He knows he should run, put as much distance as he can between himself and the oncoming troops. But something roots him in place. Maybe it's the raw desperation on the girl's face. The way she cradles her dad, whispering reassurances even as tears slip down her cheeks.

"Beautiful," he whispers, catching himself off guard. Because she is. Not in the superficial way that people chase with their nanite enhancements and designer genes. But in strength, the sheer force of will that blazes in those quicksilver eyes.

Suddenly, her gaze shifts, meeting his dead on. For a suspended moment, they just stare at each other, chests heaving, pulses pounding. A crackle of connection, of understanding, arcs between them.

Then her eyes flutter shut and she slumps over her father, spent. The helicopters descend, soldiers shouting orders. Joe knows he has to act fast.

Joe sprints forward, his mind racing almost as fast as his feet. That silver-eyed girl and her dad...He knows them. Or rather, he knows *of* them.

Dr. Rufus Melody and his daughter, Silver. The inventor of the nanite pill. The country's most revered scientist. And they are on the run just like that soldier said. Not so long ago, a million dollars would have changed everything for Joe. But not anymore. Now there isn't enough money in the world to make him turn these two people in.

"Not on my watch," Joe mutters under his breath. He reaches Silver's side as the first soldiers touch down in the clearing. Up close, her features are even more striking, simultaneously delicate and fierce. Her eyelids flutter but don't open.

"I've got you," he promises softly, scooping her up as if

she weighs nothing. She's tall, but in his massive arms she feels small. Fragile. He cradles her head against his chest.

Rufus groans, struggling to sit up. His leg is a mangled mess. Those pills might knit the bone back together, given time. But he won't be running anywhere. He meets Joe's gaze, his eyes glassy with pain but still sharp. Assessing.

"Take her," he rasps. "Please. Don't let them—"

His words cut off as he slumps back, unconscious. Joe swallows hard. He looks from the injured man to the girl in his arms, then to the soldiers fanning out between the trees, weapons raised.

Time's up. Gabbing the girl's pack, he turns and runs, Silver held tight against him. Bullets zing past his ears, but he barely flinches, trusting in his armored skin, his superhuman speed.

He doesn't let himself think beyond the next breath, the next step. He can only pray he's fast enough and strong enough to get them both away. And that his knee doesn't pick a bad time to give out.

Joe churns up the ground as he sprints through the forest, dodging trees and leaping over fallen logs without breaking his stride. Silver remains limp in his arms, her dark hair streaming behind them.

Just keep running, he tells himself. *Get her somewhere safe.*

But where is safe?

Behind him, shouts ricochet between the trees, then the crackle of numerous radios sound. The soldiers are regrouping, coordinating.

Joe risks a glance over his shoulder and immediately

wishes he hadn't. At least a dozen armored figures are crashing through the underbrush in pursuit, heavy boots trampling everything in their path. And worse—a pack of hellhounds lopes alongside them, tongue lolling between razor sharp fangs.

Shit.

His heart pounds even harder, adrenaline surging. No way can he outrun those monsters, not burdened with Silver's weight and his fatiguing knee. He needs a plan, fast.

A flash of light catches his eye and he jerks his head up. There, through a gap in the leaves, a ravine. And maybe, just maybe...

"Hang on," he mutters to the unconscious girl, gathering himself. "This is gonna get a little bumpy."

Drawing on every ounce of his enhanced strength, he leaps. Then, at the last possible second, he curls himself protectively around Silver. He holds her tight as he flies through the air, aiming for the far bank. His bulk nanites do the rest. His feet hit the ground and he keeps running through trees.

The soldiers' shouts fade away.

He doesn't stop until his knee gives out and he almost drops Silver. He stands there panting, surrounded by trees, Silver cradled in his arms, taking in the welcome sight of a semi-circle of dilapidated cabins. Only then does he collapse to his knees in the dirt, chest heaving, limbs trembling from exertion. Slowly, carefully, he lays Silver on the ground, checks her breathing. She's still out cold, but seems unharmed.

Thank God. He allows himself a few seconds to kneel

there, gazing at her perfect features slackened in sleep. Tentatively, he smooths a wayward curl from her cheek, marveling at the impossible softness of her skin.

Who is this girl, really? What secrets lie hidden behind those long lashes, that stubborn chin? He wants to know everything.

CHAPTER 8

Joe's heavy footsteps echo through the deserted cabin as he carries Silver's limp body inside. Dust motes dance in the shaft of light streaming through a broken window. He lays her gently on a ratty old couch, wincing at the dark blood staining her T-shirt.

"Hang in there, Silver," he murmurs, rummaging through her pack until he finds a roll of bandages. Peeling back the blood-soaked fabric and tearing it away from her skin, he sucks in a breath at the deep gash marring her shoulder. Must've been some fight.

Once the wound is clean and the bandage secure, Joe lines up the contents that fell out of her pack on a rotting crate: a few bottles of pills, a wicked-looking throwing knife, a battered old guitar pick. He shakes his head. "Quite the arsenal you've got here." His eyes linger on the pills—are they nanites? Just a single pill could transform someone's life. For better or worse. Funny how something so small can cause such chaos.

He finds a sleeping bag tied to her pack and lays it over her. While Silver sleeps, her breath shallow but steady, Joe builds a fire in the ancient stone chimney. Lord knows they both could use some food. He slips into the quiet woods. Before long, a fat squirrel is roasting over the crackling flames, the savory scent filling the musty cabin.

Joe settles by the hearth to wait, gaze lingering on Silver's pale face, the curve of her cheek, the elegant line of her neck, the tumble of dark hair. She is really quite beautiful.

He massages his sore knee, swollen and aching from the day's exertions, unsure if he'll be able to walk on it tomorrow, let alone run. Lost in thought, Joe almost misses the fluttering of Silver's dark lashes. Her eyes blink open, hazy and unfocused at first, before sharpening with a startling intensity. She bolts upright, wincing as the motion pulls at her wounded shoulder, and grabs her knife.

"Where's my father?"

Admiring her feistiness in spite of her injuries, Joe raises both hands. "I have no idea where your father is."

She eyes him suspiciously. "What did you do with him?"

Wanting to make her feel safe, Joe takes a few steps back. "Nothing. I swear. I think the army got him."

She frowns, then winces. "Aren't you the army?"

Joe glances at his clothes, the faded combats trousers, the khaki green T-shirt. He can see why she thinks that. "No. No *way*." He points at his trousers. "Lifted these from an unsuspecting soldier a couple days ago."

Her eyes run up and down Joe's body. He hasn't been eyed that closely since he was around the cheerleaders when he played ball. A little uncomfortable under the scrutiny, he's tempted to throw in a cocky grin and a suggestive wink. But now isn't the time for that.

"I'm not going to hurt you." He risks a few steps closer, grabs her flask from the floor and offers it to her. "Have some water."

She eyes the flask like it contains poison, then snatches it from his hand. She drinks greedily, half of it dribbling down her chin, never taking her eyes off him.

"Easy," Joe chuckles.

Silver spots the bandage wound around her shoulder, her lack of T-shirt, and her face heats.

Joe points to her shoulder. "You were injured. I needed to dress your wound." He blushes, not willing to admit how much he relished the brief glance at her curves while he was playing medic.

"Who are you?" She backs into the corner of the couch, which squeaks an irritated protest.

"Name's Rucker. Joe Rucker." Joe offers a hand, but she doesn't shake. "And you, I believe, judging by that nice little array of nanite pills, are Silver Melody."

She frowns. "How do you know who I am?"

"Everyone knows who the inventors of the nanite pills are." Joe picks up a bottle and shakes it. "And their very unadjusted daughter. More so since there's been a price on your head."

Narrowing her eyes, she wobbles to her feet. "Is that your plan? To turn me in? Is that what you did to my Dad?" She swishes the knife between them, but Joe doesn't shy away. She can't hurt him with it. She seems to realize that at the same time, drops the blade to her side, and curses under her breath.

"Of course not." Joe cocks his head. "I couldn't get to you both before the army got there. Your dad looked...pretty bad."

"You should have saved my father!" Lurching forward, she drops the knife and pounds her fist against his armored chest. Joe barely feels the impact, but a grimace passes over her lips and she cradles her fist. Without warning, she moves to sweep his legs, but Joe sees the move coming and dances out the way. Damn, she's feisty. Silver collapses on the floor, her teeth audibly smacking together. "He's more important than me."

"I'm sorry. He was beyond my limited medic skills."

A renegade tear drips down her cheek.

"Hey, it's okay." Joe touches her arm, but she leaps away from him. He raises both hands. "I didn't mean any harm."

"We'll see about that." She cowers away, cradling her knife.

"What were you and your father doing in the woods?" He keeps his voice low and soft, worried she might hightail it out of the cabin any second and run straight into the arms of the army.

She doesn't look at him, but keeps her head down.

Joe backs away, leans against a wall, and crosses one ankle over the other. He'd give anything to give her the comfort she so clearly needs, but he is a bulk in her eyes. The enemy. And so he keeps distance between them. "Do you have more clothes? Can I help you get dressed?"

She lifts her head and glares at him, then pulls the sleeping bag around her shoulders.

"Have it your way." He shrugs and returns to the fire, where he turns the sticks. The tempting aroma of meat fills the musty space.

"Where are we now?" she asks, eyeing the food.

Joe reaches for one of the sticks and hands it to her. Cautiously, she grabs it and inspects it. What does she think he's done with it? Basted it with the oh so many vials of poison he carries with him on the run? She's even more cynical than him. Joe laughs as he takes another of the sticks and gulps the sliver of meat down in one. Finally, she nibbles the edge of hers.

"Some kind of abandoned village. A couple of ramshackle houses." Joe smiles, attempting to put her at ease. He can't imagine how hard life has been for her. Especially after her mother was arrested. And God knows what she faced in the forest. At least one hellhound, that's for sure. She doesn't need a bulk dressed in army fatigues adding to her misery. "Look at least a hundred years old."

"They are." She stares at him, taking him in. "That's not where you attacked me."

Chuckling, Joe rolls his eyes. "I didn't attack you. I *saved* you." He kneels next to the crate. "I carried you here."

"All this way? And my rucksack?" she asks, glancing at it.

Joe nods. "I saw the hellhound. You managed to kill it?"

It's her turn to nod.

"How? I had a run-in with one. It's one of the few times I've been thankful for my impenetrable skin. It kept coming for me until I managed to strangle it."

"I didn't have a choice. It was eating my father." She

fiddles with the empty stick in her hand. "It would have killed us both."

Holy shit. She took out a hellhound with one measly knife? On her own? With no enhancement? He read somewhere that she is proficient in karate. But still. Joe gives her another once over. There's more to Silver Melody than meets the eyes.

She reaches for her rucksack and removes a new T-shirt. Unable to slip her injured arm into the right hole, Joe moves to help her, but she shoots him a glare.

He steps back. "Just trying to help."

"Uh-huh."

Wincing, she slips the shirt over her head. Then she reaches for one of the pill bottles, shakes out two and swallows them. Is she an unadjusted turned nanite junkie? That would explain the hellhound. But if she's so in to nanites, it doesn't explain why she's running, or why the army is after her. Maybe it's one of those temporary ones. Joe eyes the bottle.

Regeneration.

He raises both brows. It is the very thing he's been searching for, for months. Right there. It would fix everything. He could go back to football...

Except there is no more football. There is only the resistance and finding his parents.

She's not a junkie, she just wants to cure her injury. When Joe refocuses his attention on Silver, her eyelids are drooping.

"What did you say about a price on my head?" she whispers.

"You and your father are wanted. It's a lot of money..." He trails off as she falls asleep.

Exhausted by all the running and with an ache settling deep into his knee, Joe stretches out on the floor on his sleeping mat. He tries to get comfortable, but the pain in his knee is enough to keep him awake.

A couple hours later, he becomes aware of small movements from Silver. She rustles through her bag. Swings her legs to the floor. Tiptoes toward the door. Doesn't she know how dangerous it is for her out there?

As she steps past him, he circles his hand around her boot. "Where do you think you're going?"

She tries to kick him off, but Joe's grip is firm. "So, I'm a prisoner?"

He releases her and springs to his feet. "You're injured. You need to rest."

She pulls back the collar of her shirt and shows him the healed wound.

He looks from her shoulder to her face. Twice. He didn't know regeneration pills worked that quickly. "Well, I never."

"I need to find my Dad." She turns toward the door.

"You know," he calls after her, "a lot of people are looking for you out there. President Bear put a million dollars on your head. And your father's. Each. That's a lot of money to a lot of people."

"A million dollars?" She gulps. "That is a lot of money."

"Yeah. I could buy a regeneration pill with that. Several." He wants one of those pills so badly. But he's not a thief. And there might be others who need it more than him.

She edges closer to the door. "Why do you need a regeneration pill?"

"I was recruited for the NFL. I'd only been playing for six months when I tore my ACL. My insurance package didn't cover regeneration pills, so they dropped me." The anger washes over him.

She sizes him up, as if trying to make a decision. "And then what?"

Joe shrugs. "And then, nothing. I argued my case in court but didn't get anywhere. Got disillusioned. Then I heard about the cave—"

She freezes. "How do you know about the cave?"

"Ran into a friend in a similar predicament. He told me about a safe place, and with my parents in a compound..." He shakes his head. "There's no place else for me to go."

Her expression hardens, those silver eyes turning to steel. "What compounds?"

He frowns. "You don't know?"

"No."

"The army and the City Investigation Force have rounded up all the unadjusteds in the country and detained them in compounds."

"To force the nanites down their throats?"

"To start with, but then they got a little desperate." Joe leans against the wall. "With unadjusteds fleeing all over the city, hell, all over the country, it had an effect on the superbeings."

"Alts," she mutters.

"Whatever you want to call us." He schools his expression, but the jab hurts a little.

She hovers by the door. "What happened?"

"The adjusteds went a little wild."

"Wild how?"

"No one knows. They started killing each other. Like, rampage bad." Joe thinks of the woman he saved in the street. "There's a whole ton of speculation. Some of the superbeings who've taken only one nanite, like me, seem fine. But any more than that, they went bad. The only thing keeping them in control is the presence of the unadjusteds."

"I don't understand."

"Neither do I," Joe says. "That's all I got before..." *before he killed the soldier.* "But my parents are unadjusted. They poured all their money into that one nanite so I could have a career. Now they're in a compound." His voice hardens. "And I, for one, am going to get them the hell out."

"Well, good luck with that." She turns and yanks the door open.

Joe steps across the room. "Where are you going?"

"I already told you, I'm going to get my dad."

"You don't even know where he is."

She cocks a defensive shoulder. "I'll go to the caves first. Get Matt to help me."

Joe's chest blooms with pain on her behalf. "Matt?"

She glances over her shoulder at him through the doorway. "He's my best friend."

"I think he's the one I've been hearing about, helping to organize the resistance." Joe closes the gap between them. "We're going to the same place. We might as well go together."

"I'm okay on my own." She slams the door in his face.

"For fuck's sake," Joe mutters as he grabs his belongings and hurries after her.

He doesn't want to freak her out, so he keeps a little distance between them, but it's harder than it seems. Although his vison is enhanced, it's not any better than the average unadjusted at night. He can't see shit and she is widening her lead.

The forest around them falls silent as he thunders through bushes and swears at the branches invisible in the shadows. Of all the asininely stupid things to do, to go wandering in a forest at night with hellhounds and the army around...After half an hour, he loses her completely. Thinking he's got her trail, he forges ahead, until her voice sounds from the darkness and scares the crap out of him.

"If you're going to follow me, you really need to be quiet."

Joe yelps and trips over her feet.

She's waiting against a tree, using the knife to pick dirt from her fingernails.

He pushes himself up. "Damn, Silver. How can you see where you're going? There's no moon tonight."

She removes a bottle of pills from her pack and places one in his palm. Heart thudding, he rolls it between his fingertips. "What is it?"

"Night vision."

"I thought you were an unadjusted."

"Of course I am. I'd never...they're temporary. It lasts a few days."

"I'm not sure I want to take this. Superbeings are going murderous because they're taking too many nanites. As irritating as you are, I'm not sure I want to murder you. Yet," he grits out.

"Hmm. I'm harder to kill than I look." She tosses her hair over her shoulder, and her silver eyes glint in the darkness. "But you don't need to worry, it'll wear off soon enough."

"Thanks." Even though he has impenetrable skin, there are nasties in the woods he doesn't want to meet again. He wants to be able to see what's coming at him. Joe dumps his pack on the ground, uncorks his water flask and swallows the pill. "How long does it take to...oh my!" He cranes his neck around the tree and peers into the darkness of the forest. It's like it's noon. He can see *everything*. Even the fox diving into its burrow. There, a pair of glowing eyes, low to the ground, hopefully nothing to worry about. A bat streaking between the trees. A squirrel nibbling on a nut. "I'm not sure I want to see what I'm seeing. There are so many animals out here."

"Surely a big, bad bulk like you isn't afraid of a prowling fox?"

Refusing to rise to her jibe, Joe re-shoulders his pack. "There are more than foxes in the woods."

Joe doesn't miss it when her hand floats to her knife. She's afraid, but she's hiding it well.

She pulls out a compass and points in a direction. Joe follows her, glad of the company—even if she isn't warm and fuzzy—and is relieved she knows where she's going. But with all the running and saving making his knee throb like he's got a spike in the joint, he's wincing with every step.

When the sky lightens and the nocturnal animals return to their lairs, Joe sits on the ground and gulps from his flask. A mixture of sweat and frustration beads on his face. His knee will no longer bend to his command.

"What's the problem?" Silver asks.

"It's my knee. All the walking." He presses around the joint.

She plucks a bottle of pills from her pack and chucks him a tablet. He catches it in his palm and stares at the damn thing.

"Is this going to kill me?" he asks, staring at the pill.

"Maybe." She chuckles.

He locks his eyes onto her. Can he trust her?

She smiles. A smile of such warmth that Joe's boundaries fall away. "It's not going to kill you. It'll help your injury. I promise."

Joe doesn't move his gaze from her face. It's a regeneration pill. In his hand. The very thing he's been seeking. Thousands of dollars worth of. The answer to all his dreams. And woes.

He squints at her. "How do I know I can trust you?"

She barks out a laugh. "Take it, or don't take it. Up to you."

He nods, then swallows the pill. Just like that.

It isn't long before a tingling sensation spreads through his knee. A gentle heat. A subtle pressure. He waits it out.

She sits next to him on the trunk, bringing the smell of pine and earth and scents that Joe never wants to stop smelling. There is something about her that is dangerous and feminine and vulnerable and captivating all at the same time. And he can't take his eyes off her silver irises.

Feeling the heat of a blush, Joe averts his gaze and

rummages in his bag for the squirrel meat he secured. It's running low, but he's happy to share. They're in this together now. "I don't know how I can ever repay you."

Silver taps her finger against the blade of her knife. "Just don't make me regret my decision."

An hour later, Joe stands. There is no twinge in his knee, no stiffness, no heat, no pull of ligaments. He frowns, stares at his joint. He can't remember what it felt like to have a functioning knee.

"What's wrong?"

"My knee. It doesn't hurt." He bends and flexes his leg a couple of times, performs a few low squats, and dances around the forest, leaping over ferns.

"Well, that's a good thing then." Silver claps.

He whoops and yells at the trees and thanks Heaven and God above. This is the best day of his entire life. Even better than when he got his contract through.

"God and Heaven had nothing to do with it," she calls after him.

Joe runs back to Silver and crouches so they're eye level. "Thank you."

And he means it. Silver just changed his life. And he owes her. Big time. He will help her. He will protect her. Damn, he'll help her get her father back too. And not just because he owes her, but because he wants to. He's never met anyone so determined, so feisty, so damn beautiful.

Read on to read the first chapter of the next instalment, *Erica Swiftfield...*

⋙⋘

Thank you so much for making it all the way to the end. I hope you have enjoyed Joe's companion novella and are excited to discover the rest of the series. If you did, leaving a review is the best possible present for an author!

You can do it here: https://geni.us/JoeRucker

⋙⋘

If you want to know what happens to Silver and Joe during their ongoing journey, don't forget to check out *The Unadjusteds*:

https://geni.us/Theunadjusteds

If you want to experience more of my books, do join my Facebook readers group where you can chat to other readers and discuss my books, as well as anything else you are reading. I am very active in this group, and you can expect book jokes, puzzles, riddles, quizzes, giveaways, the opportunity to name characters, as well as secret information about what I'm working on, cover reveals and so much more!

Just click here:
https://www.facebook.com/groups/840324970233576

FREEBIE

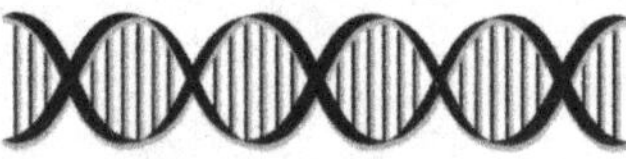

If you'd like to read the next book in the series for FREE, please sign up to my newsletter at

https://www.marisanoelle.com/subscribe/

And don't forget there are 10 more companion novellas in the series:

Silver Melody
Matt Lawson
Erica Swiftfield
Paige Starling
Hal Small
Kyle Lewis
Jacob Shea
Sawyer Watson
Addison Shields
President Bear

Read on to read the first chapter of the next instalment, *Erica Swiftfield...*

ERICA SWIFTFIELD

An Unadjusteds Story

MARISA NOELLE

Butterfly wings made Erica Swiftfield the most popular girl in high school, until she made a disastrous decision...

For years, Erica dreamed of being "adjusted," of leaving her ordinary self behind. With her newfound wings given to her on her fourteenth birthday, her popularity soars and she sets her sights on head cheerleader. But when a tragic accident claims her best friend's life, Erica's perfect image shatters. Consumed by guilt and struggling to piece herself back together, she learns that perfection has a cost—and she might not be the only one paying it.

Soon after, the president declares every unadjusted citizen must take a gene-altering pill or face "unfortunate circumstances." No longer clear which side she's on, Erica is thrust into a movement led by The Unadjusteds, a group of rebels fighting for autonomy. Their world is dangerous, and fighting for them goes against everything

Erica thought she believed—but it might also be the key to her redemption.

In a world obsessed with altering the human body, Erica must decide: Will she fight to protect others from becoming pawns of perfection, or will she lose herself in the pursuit of it?

Read on for first chapter...

CHAPTER ONE

THE THOUGHT CIRCLES Erica's brain with more aggression than a bulk crashing into a human opponent on the field. It's been on her mind all day. Through Maths with Mr. Reynolds and his malfunctioning EmotionAmp ring that makes everyone in a ten-foot radius drowsy, through recess when she nibbles on a few slices of apple, through dance practice when she falls off the top of the pyramid and bruises her button nose on the crash mats. That wouldn't have happened if she had wings.

If her mom and dad haven't reneged on their promise, that small box she eyed on the coffee table this morning is the answer to her dreams.

Erica and Jess burst through the front door, laughter trailing behind them like confetti. Arms brimming with a precarious stack of snacks, they tumble into the hallway and make a beeline for the living room.

"I still can't believe you convinced your mom to let you

open presents without her," Jess says, her warm smile whipping Erica's excitement higher.

Jess' orange wings flutter as she sets the gifts on the coffee table. Wings she's had for over a year, because her parents agreed thirteen was the right age for butterfly wings. Erica wouldn't choose orange—the garish color makes her look more sickly than beautiful—but they suit her girlfriend. Most of the time. Erica knows when to keep her mouth shut. When the right time is to tell a friend if their ass looks too big in a pair of skinny jeans or if hooking up with three guys in one night will cause the rumor mill to explode. And Jess' wings have kind of grown on her, outlined in thick, black lacing that makes the colors pop, and accented with swirling EcoTattoos. Since the transformation, Jess sticks to wearing mostly orange and black and a few other neutral tones to set the wings off. That's one thing Jess does well; fashion. And let's face it, she didn't choose the orange. It was one of the cheaper nanites, and the cheaper nanites don't come with choices. But at least she has the wings. At least *she* will make the cheer squad in high school next semester. Erica tries not to let the envy get to her. It's her fourteenth birthday after all, and if things go right, she'll be getting her own pair of wings. Purple ones.

Erica shrugs, a sly grin playing at her lips. "She knows I'm impatient. Plus, she had to fly out for that conference, so it was open them alone or—" she makes a pitiful puppy dog face "—open them with my best friend here."

Jess raises an eyebrow. "*Best friend?*"

A flush warms Erica's face. Their relationship is new. They evolved past the friend zone a couple months ago, but she hasn't told anyone yet. Her parents aren't quite as accepting as Jess'. And they might force a nanite on her. The wrong kind. The kind that might take her feelings away.

Erica leans over and places a soft kiss on Jess' lips.

"That's better," Jess says, punching her lightly on the shoulder. "But you're still spoiled."

"Maybe a little," Erica admits, plopping onto the couch and ripping into a bag of chips. She offers them to Jess, who takes a few and sits cross-legged on the floor. "But I'm grateful, you know. For everything."

"Especially for these!" Jess holds up a sparkly box, shaking it gently. "You're going to love what I got you."

"Gimme!"

Jess holds the box out of reach. Laughing, Erica clambers over her, pins her to the floor, and snatches the box from her hand, the chips spilling over the floor.

Jess giggles, that adorable high-pitched laugh that makes Erica's stomach feel warm and cozy. "Okay, you win!"

Erica leans forward as Jess opens the box just enough for Erica to see inside. Her eyes widen and she clasps her hands over her mouth. "No way! Jess, these are amazing!"

"I knew you'd like them," Jess says, lifting the earrings out of the box. They are iridescent and purple. *Purple.* Like her wings are going to be. "They're HoloGems."

Erica's mouth drops open. "No way!" She scrambles for the earrings, slides one into the hole in her ear, and immediately, tiny fluttering butterflies are projected flying around her head. "Best. Present. Ever!" She plants another kiss on Jess' lips, soaking in the warmth of her mouth, the feel of her skin tingling against hers. "Thank you, Jess."

"You're welcome." Jess stands and flutters her wings. "So, where is it? Are you going to open it?"

Erica eyes the small purple box her mom wrapped late last night. She thinks it contains a nanite. The answer to her dreams. And her popularity. And her existence. But then she remembers the kid who died last month when he took a bulk nanite. He wanted to be a football player. His body didn't take to the change. It happens sometimes.

"I will," Erica replies, twirling a strand of her long, dark hair around her finger. "But I want to ask you a question first..."

"Okay. Shoot. What's up?"

"Was it scary? The transformation? Did it hurt?"

Jess shrugs. "A little scary. But mostly exciting. It didn't hurt. Are you having doubts? Because if you don't want to, you don't have to."

"No doubts..." Erica bites her lip, her mind racing with possibilities. "It's just a big change. I have a low pain threshold. And I won't be able to wear that purple sweater anymore...no wing slits."

Jess laughs. "I know an alteration place. It will look even better than before."

Why is she hesitating? Wings are the only thing she's wanted for years. Not only so she'll be guaranteed a spot on the high school cheerleading team next year, but so she can fly away. Go wherever she wants. Somewhere private. Somewhere she and Jess can be alone and they won't have to worry about being seen.

Jess sits again, puts a hand on hers. "You know I'll support you no matter what, right?"

"I know," Erica says, softer now. "It's just a lot to think about."

Their fingers brush as Jess hands Erica another gift, and a spark of anticipation ignites in Erica's chest.

Jess stretches her arms above her head, then playfully flutters her orange wings. The iridescent sheen catches the light, making her look like a living flame. Erica can't help but stare; the wings have always fascinated her, especially since she added the swirling digital tattoos.

"Do they feel...real?" Erica asks, dropping the unopened gift, and Jess pauses mid-flutter.

Jess grins, turning to give Erica a full view of the delicate structures. "Touch them and find out."

Erica reaches out tentatively, her fingertips grazing the edge of one wing, an EcoTattoo vanishing from under her fingertips only to reappear in a different section of the wing. It's softer than she expected, like the finest silk, yet it holds a surprising amount of warmth. She snatches her hand back, as if she's stroked a live wire.

"It feels like I've always had them," Jess says, her voice filled with pride.

Erica sinks deeper into the couch, her thoughts drifting. "It's so crazy to think a little pill can do all that."

"It's not just a pill," Jess says, sitting next to Erica. "It's a whole process. You have to be ready for it, mind and body. The change isn't instant."

"How long did it take for you?"

Jess tilts her head, thinking. "About a month for the wings to fully grow in. But every day I could feel them. And I practiced in MetaMorph so I could fly as soon as the wings were strong enough."

Erica nods. She's clocked so many hours in the virtual reality setting that she's earned herself a bonus EmotionAmp ring. "And you never had second thoughts?"

Jess laces their fingers together. "Oh, tons. But I knew this was what I wanted. And it's not like I could go back once I started."

Erica shifts on the couch, projected purple butterflies roaming around her head. "That's the scary part, isn't it? Being stuck with the change. Did you see that guy with the hedgehog spikes the other day?"

Jess clamps a hand over her mouth, muffling her laugh. "And the woman with the turtle shell on her back?"

Erica shakes her head. "That's what you get in the discount aisle, I guess."

Jess cups her face, brushes a thumb over her cheek. "But you know you're getting the real deal. There's nothing to worry about. I'll be right here with you. If it's what you truly want."

Erica nods, picturing what people will say when they see her at school on Monday. The stares, the gasps, the gossip, the admiration. She craves it all. Erica holds Jess' gaze. She remembers when Jess was just another pretty girl in school, popular but not exceptional. The wings had transformed her, yes, but it was more than just a physical change. Jess had an aura now, a confidence that was unshakable.

"You don't have to take it today," Jess says. "You can wait."

Erica arches an eyebrow. "Tryouts are in a few weeks.

You think I'm going to let you be in line for head cheerleader? Nuh-uh—we share, remember?"

Jess laughs. "Oh my God. You are the most competitive person I know."

"Gotta be in it to win it." Erica picks up the sparkly box Jess gave her earlier and slides the other earring into her ear. Now it's a butterfly party, the tiny holographic creatures fluttering over her head and down her arms, their wings changing color in pleasing hues. Soon, she'll fly with them.

Jess' eyes soften. "Happy birthday, Erica."

Jess is about to kiss her when Erica's phone rings.

"Hey, Mom," she answers, her voice cautious.

Jess gives her wide eyes. Beautiful brown eyes that melt her heart.

"Erica, darling, how are you?" Her mother's voice crackles through the speaker, warm but distant. "I'm so sorry I haven't called sooner. This conference has been non-stop."

"I'm good," Erica says. "How's Boston?"

"Humid. I don't have long. Wanted to check in on your... transformation. Have you taken the pill yet? Is Sarah there with you? You know you can wait until I get home—"

"I'm good," Erica cuts her off. Sarah is her best friend, Jess is her girlfriend, Erica's mother doesn't need to know that it's Jess who is with her. "I haven't taken it yet. I'm working up to it."

"You can always wait for your dad—"

"No way." Erica rolls her eyes and Jess laughs. "He wanted me to get hawk wings, for God's sake. I mean brown? Really?"

"They *are* more powerful..." Her mom lowers her voice.

"I thought about getting a nanite for myself. I'm thinking blue wings. Maybe with my next bonus money."

Something tightens in Erica' s chest. The wings are her idea. Her mother never professed to be interested in nanites until now. This is Erica's dream. And she doesn't want to share it. Doesn't want to see her mother living out failed cheerleading dreams through a pair of wings.

"We could fly to the beach together..." her mom babbles on. Doesn't she know butterfly wings aren't made for endurance? The beach is miles away. States away.

"I've gotta go, Mom," Erica says. "More presents to open."

"Well, okay darling, happy birthday."

Erica disconnects the call. She picks up the purple box from the coffee table and slides it open. Inside is a tiny white pill. Erica puts it in her mouth and swallows it with a sip of soda.

If you want to carry on reading, click here:
https://geni.us/EricaSwiftfield